WEREWOLF ACADEMY: YEAR FOUR

JAYME MORSE

JODY MORSE

CHAPTER 1

$\mathcal{A}$ s I sat on the white fur-covered stool in front of the vanity in my bedroom, I stared at myself in the mirror. My long golden blonde hair fell over my shoulders in loose curls. I wore the same purple smokey eyeshadow look I normally wore, my eyes were framed by black eyeliner, and my lashes were coated in multiple coats of mascara.

On the outside, nothing about me had changed. I still looked the same as I always did, except I knew that I was different.

I was changed.

And it wasn't only just *me* who had changed. *Everything* had changed.

Almost everything that had become so familiar to me had shifted.

Under ordinary circumstances, I would have been getting ready to start my senior year at Werewolf Academy. I would have been driving my mates nuts because I would have taken way too long to achieve the perfect back to school look.

Two years ago today, I had been fighting with Theo. One year ago today, we had been getting ready for school... together. That thought made me feel numb inside.

The thing was, that was all in the past. So much had changed since then, and there was nothing I could even do about it.

Nothing about this year was ordinary, and it was about to get a whole lot weirder.

Werewolf Academy had shut down for the semester, and possibly the year. All of our classes were being held virtually.

Not taking classes on campus was weird in itself, but even worse than that, students were dying. Every few days, I received news in my Werewolf Academy email inbox that another student's life had been lost. I wasn't sure how many familiar faces I would see when we *did* finally go back to Werewolf Academy.

No one had any idea how long it would take before we could return. Headmaster Black would reevaluate the situation in December, but as of right now, things weren't looking so good.

We were in the middle of a war—the war between the paranormal races. It had begun just days after the end of the year carnival at Werewolf Academy. The vision that Gloria and I had seen had been right; Iris and Milos Santorini had started the fires that were still going in Wolflandia, and the paranormal world war had begun a week later.

The day after the fires began, my mates, my friends,

and I had fled to Nocturne Island, the island that was going to be our home for the indefinite future. It was the island where I belonged... *sort of.*

Don't get me wrong. The island was beautiful. I had explored every inch of it. The beach spanned for miles and there was a village with cobblestone roads and cottages, along with a forest and farmland. But it just didn't feel like home.

I wasn't sure if it ever really would. We had been on Nocturne Island for five months, but instead of feeling happy and content, it still made me feel nauseous most of the time.

Not that my current predicament helped with the nausea, I thought to myself.

But even though it didn't feel like home and the place made me sick, I still lived in the castle. Yes, the castle, because I was about to ascend the throne.

It had taken some convincing on Gloria's behalf to persuade the werewolves who ran the museum that I was Princess Fallyn. After a lot of convincing, they ran some DNA tests, which had proved that it was true. Not that I had needed the proof myself; I'd had enough visions of my past life as Princess Fallyn to know that it was true. But the DNA tests had confirmed it for all of us, myself included, once and for all.

I had been born to be the next Queen of the wolves.

Given who I was, we all knew that there was a high risk of Nocturne Island getting attacked if anyone figured out where we were. And considering Milos was able to figure out my location at any given time, Gloria had known that we'd needed to do something to protect me.

The most obvious solution had been hiding Nocturne Island—not just from Milos and Iris, but from *everyone*. My life was at a much greater risk now that it was well-known throughout the werewolf world that I was the long-lost princess. We had to worry about other were-wolves wanting to harm me, as well as paranormal beings from other races.

Being princess came with its drawbacks, to say the least.

So, to keep me protected, Gloria had rounded up some of the most powerful witches in the world to put a veil over the island. The veil had completely hidden the island; no one could locate it by boat or by plane. It just made the island appear as though it was a part of the ocean that surrounded it.

Even though my mates all seemed to think the plan was genius, the truth was that I didn't trust it. I was afraid that someone would be able to figure out a way to undo the spell and remove the veil, that Milos would find us. The fear kept me up late at night, and even when I was able to fall asleep, I often had nightmares about it—nightmares that sometimes woke me up screaming.

Every night, one of my mates slept with me. I needed someone to be there, to console me. Even though I was about to become a powerful Queen, the truth was that I still felt like I was in constant need of their protection.

I knew I needed to stop worrying about what the future held. With the veil, we were safe… for now.

Well, *most* of us were safe, that is.

I still missed Theo every single day since Milos had killed him. From the moment the silver bullet had stopped his heart from beating, it felt like a part of me had died with him. But life had been moving at high-speed, so fast that I didn't feel like I had really had the chance to grieve his death. I'd had to put on my brave face and be strong, even though the truth was that I felt anything *but* strong. Most of the time, I just wanted to lock myself away in my bedroom quarters and cry myself to sleep. I wanted to cry until I had been completely drained of tears.

But no one wanted a weak Queen, and that was exactly what I was about to become. I wasn't strong or brave, or as cold-hearted as I needed to be, by any means. But I needed to keep that detail to myself. I wasn't about to let anyone know the truth about how weak I was. So, even though I wanted to cry my eyes out just about every day, I didn't.

Instead, I had been trying to master my poker face. Every day, I put a brave face on, trying to make it through the day as I silently felt my heart breaking in ways that I couldn't even begin to explain.

This was one of those days where, more than ever, I needed to put a brave face on. I felt Theo's absence even more than I normally did.

"Raven, are you ready now?" Maddie asked from behind me then.

I glanced over at her. She wore her long black hair in a fancy updo on top of her head with a few loose curls in the front, and she was donning the light pink, lacy brides-maid dress she had picked out for herself to wear. The high-low style made her tan legs look even longer, and the off-the-shoulder sleeves made her look like she had

5

fallen out of a book of fairytales. She had done a much better job at choosing a dress for herself than I ever could have... especially in my current state of mind.

"Yeah."

As ready as I would ever be, anyway, I thought as I met my eyes in the mirror one more time.

"You look absolutely gorgeous, honey," Vince said as he entered the room, wearing the pink tux Maddie had picked out for him to be my bridesman. It was a few shades darker than her dress.

Vince had added a few bright pink highlights to his hair, which he wore spiky in the front, to complement the dress.

"Thanks," I replied, not fully believing it myself. I rose to my feet, eyeing myself in the floor-length mirror that hung from the wall.

The dress was the whitest of white with silver sparkly sequins adorned at the bust. The dress hugged my curves in all of the right places before flowing out into a poofy princess style.

It was a pretty wedding gown, but honestly? It wasn't what I would have picked out for myself.

It just didn't feel like *me*, at all. If anything, I just felt kind of uncomfortable in the dress Maddie had chosen for me.

There wasn't anything *wrong* with it, it just felt like a dress that someone else should have been wearing.

I had been too depressed about Theo's death to plan the wedding, so I had pretty much left everything up to Maddie. She had been excited, of course, to plan every single detail of a Royal wedding. The truth was that the photos from today would go down in history. It was the first historical wedding that had taken place on Nocturne Island in hundreds of years. Even more than that, it was the first Royal wedding the werewolf world had ever seen, because the last King and Queen had had been crowned *before* the curse had turned into werewolves.

I was talking about my biological parents—the first Queen and King of the wolves, who had given birth to the first werewolf to have ever been born naturally. That would be me.

According to the legends, the King and Queen had died from the virus that had wiped out the majority of the ancient werewolf population or they had been killed by the vampires who had ambushed the castle. I didn't believe the second theory, of course, since legend had it that the vampires had completely drained me of my blood, when that obviously hadn't been the case.

No matter how the King and Queen had died, though, the castle had remained vacant for years. That was why it had taken some convincing for the museum owners to fully believe that I was, in fact, the rightful heiress to the throne.

Gloria had to tell them about the visions she had been having. They had needed to understand that me being Queen of the wolves was essential for us to have any shot in hell at winning the war that had already begun between the paranormal races.

The museum owners had finally given up their owner-ship of the castle and agreed to reinstate the palace as the royal palace—to let me become Queen.

But there was an unwritten rule about becoming the

next Queen of the wolves, one that had been around since the ancient times.

One that they hadn't been willing to change for me.

I had to take a husband.

The truth? I knew this should have been an exciting thing for me to experience. I had the chance to marry the man of my dreams in a fancy royal wedding that any girl would have dreamed about, but instead of looking forward to this day, I had actually been dreading it.

I knew that this wasn't the right time for any of that. I wasn't ready to choose just *one* of my mates to marry. There was a part of me that wished I could marry all of them. Choosing which of my mates I wanted to marry, which of my mates I wanted to make King, was hard enough. But having to do it so soon after losing one of my five mates for good only made the decision even more complicated.

I had a feeling that things would have been different if Theo was alive. I was pretty sure there was a good chance that it was him who I would have been getting ready to walk down the aisle to, that he was the one who I would have chosen to rule alongside me. I was pretty sure that he would have been my ideal King—and my ideal husband.

But that option had been torn away from me.

Instead, I had chosen the mate who I'd believed would make the next best King. All four of my mates were incredibly strong and powerful. All four of them would have made excellent kings. And yet, my head had told me which one of them to marry. My head had told me that one of them would have made the best King. And so, that was who I had chosen to marry—not because I loved any of them less than I loved him, because that wasn't the case at all. I loved *all of them*, which made it harder, in a way, to do this.

Not that it was going to change anything. It was all just a transaction, in a way. Nothing would change between the rest of us. We would still go on as usual, but still, I wondered if the rest of them were going to feel insulted that I didn't choose them to marry, to be my King.

"We should really get going," Maddie said, her voice slicing through my thoughts. "We're going to be late."

"*Fashionably* late," Vince corrected. "It's always good for the bride to make a grand entrance."

Under ordinary circumstances, I totally would have completely agreed with him. I was all about being fashionably late most of the time. But this time?

Well, this time, I was ready to just get this over with.

"Let's get this show on the road," I said as I clipped my veil into my hair.

Maddie and Vince headed for the door, and I glanced over my shoulder at my bedroom quarters. The Queen's bedroom quarters.

I was about to give up everything: my life as a single, unmarried ordinary teenager—well, as ordinary as it could possibly get for a werewolf teenager, that is. And even though I was going to keep the name Raven, I also sort of felt like I was about to give her up in a way, too.

It was all about what Raven Gallagher represented to me. It obviously wasn't the name I had been born with, but it was a big part of me and who I was. It meant so much to me.

9

Raven Gallagher symbolized my human life. It represented my parents, the ones who had raised me to believe that I was their own. It represented the life I'd had before I had met all five of my mates, before I had even known that I was a werewolf at all.

It represented Theo, a voice whispered at the back of my mind. The first time I had ever met him, I hadn't known that I had ever been anyone *but* Raven Gallagher, nor had he or the rest of the Darken. We had uncovered, over time, that I was Princess Fallyn.

So, even though my name was going to stay once I became Queen, I also couldn't help but feel like I was about to leave behind Raven Gallagher, in a huge way. I was about to close that chapter of my life—the human chapter—for good.

No, the name Raven would stay, but the truth was that I was about to embrace the ancient within me. I was about to give into my life as Fallyn, the ancient werewolf princess I had been born as, was always destined to have. The ancient werewolf princess who was about to become Queen.

The Queen who Theo would never know.

I forced back the tears. I couldn't think of him right now.

Right now, I had to get ready to embark on this new journey. I couldn't take on my new roles as wife and Queen with tears streaming down my cheeks. Everyone would be watching.

Following my friends down the hallway, I could already hear the sound of "Canon in D" beginning to fill the air.

As we reached the door that led into the castle's cathedral, Vince gave me a kiss on the cheek. "Break a leg."

"Don't tell her that! You're completely jinxing her," Maddie hissed at him. Then, putting on her best smile with her glossy pink lips, she opened the door and began to walk down the aisle.

Vince followed after her.

I heard the crowd all rise to their feet.

It was going to be so hard to face my other three mates. Even though I knew that they understood that I'd had to make a decision, I was pretty sure that none of them actually *liked* my decision. All four of them had wanted to marry me. All four of them had been ready and waiting to become my King.

I wished that I could change it. More than anything, I wished that there were four of me—one for each of them.

If only.

Instead, I was going to marry him—and *only* him—while the others watched.

I was thankful for the locket that I wore around my neck—the one that contained the herbal concoction that prevented my mates from being able to listen in on my thoughts. I wore it all the time lately, but I felt like I needed today more than ever. The last thing I wanted was for my mates to be able to hear my thoughts on my wedding day.

My fiancé stood at the end of the aisle waiting for me, his eyes pouring into mine from across the room.

Deep down, I knew that this marriage was all just part of a contract; it was a way for me to become Queen. But that didn't stop my heart from feeling... *things.*

The way he looked at me... Well, it was like I was the only one in the room. It was like *we* were the only ones in the room, like no one else was in the cathedral around us.

It was almost as if my other mates weren't even there. Even though I was aware of their presence and that they were watching me, I also couldn't bring myself to look at them. I knew that I wouldn't be able to keep it together if any of them had a sad look in their eyes. As it was, I already felt a little guilty.

There was also the fact that I couldn't bring myself to break my gaze with him... my King.

I had almost approached him when I felt it.

It was only the second time I had felt it. The first time, it had been the faintest feeling in my stomach, almost like a flutter.

This time, it was sharper. Harder. A moment later, it was followed by the slightest bit of pain, and somehow, I just *knew* what it was.

It was the baby kicking.

At that moment, I heard a clap of thunder and saw a flash of lightning, which lit up the entire cathedral.

I couldn't help but think that it was really odd that I had just felt the baby kick for the first time ever, and it had ignited lightning.

I was pretty sure that I must have only been imagining it. It had to have been nothing but an odd coincidence. We may have lived in a paranormal realm, but I had never heard of kicking babies triggering lightning and thunderstorms.

My unborn baby was going to be a werewolf, not a magician.

But the nagging thought at the back of my mind wouldn't stop reminding me that we had checked the weather forecast earlier that day and there hadn't been any storms coming.

As I had nearly reached the end of the aisle, the door to the cathedral opened, and a short man who I didn't even recognize shouted, "The veil has been lifted!"

Fuck.

I knew exactly what that meant.

We were under attack.

And I already knew exactly who was attacking us.

Milos Santorini.

CHAPTER 2

*A*s I heard the sound of shots being fired off in the distance, I stood there, completely frozen in place in front of all of my guests. *Our* guests.

My fears of Milos finding us and lifting the veil had come true. Deep down, I had known that he would find me one day, but I hadn't expected that it would fall on my wedding day.

I hadn't thought that he would try to ruin this day, like he had ruined so many other days.

It almost seemed intentional, but I knew there was no way that it could have been. Milos had no idea that we were getting married today. We hadn't let anyone off of Nocturne Island know that the Royal wedding was taking place today. We would send photos to Wolflandia, the mainland where the majority of werewolves in this realm lived, after it was over. But we had decided to keep the news under wraps.

Unless someone from Nocturne Island had allowed the news to leak out.

WEREWOLF ACADEMY: YEAR FOUR

Even though Milos had been able to get inside my mind, Gloria had done a spell that prevented him from seeing everything. Was it possible that the spell hadn't actually worked, and Milos had been watching my every move?

There was another flash of lightning. Now I knew that the thunder and lightning had nothing to do with the baby I was carrying. No, it was Milos using his dark magic to make his presence known.

Talk about a grand entrance.

As it thundered again, shivers began to make their way through me. And to top it all off, I couldn't get my feet to carry me the rest of the way towards my future husband.

That wasn't good. As their future Queen, I knew that most of our guests' eyes had to have been on me as they looked for my direction.

Truthfully, I wasn't even sure what that meant for this situation.

Milos finding us meant that the wedding was cancelled... didn't it?

I couldn't imagine us spending our time doing this whole wedding thing when we should have been rounding up an army or doing something to stop him. I wasn't even sure what the next steps were supposed to have been.

I needed the guys. I needed *all* of them. I needed Theo, but that was obviously out of the question.

I decided to risk losing what composure I did have left. I turned my head, searching for my mates in the sea of guests.

I only found one.

Rhys stood with his arms crossed against one wall, between the windows. He nodded in my direction and shot me a tight smile.

He didn't look happy, but I couldn't tell if it was because I wasn't marrying him, or if it was because Milos was here.

Scanning the crowd, I glanced around for the other Darken guys, but I didn't see them.

Where the hell were my other mates?

I turned my head back towards the altar and locked eyes with my fiancé then.

Concern filled his green irises as he stared back at me.

He took a few steps toward me and held out his arm. I hooked my hand through it and allowed him to lead me to the altar, even though it was beginning to feel like the room around us was closing in on me. I could feel myself starting to hyperventilate. I was afraid I was going to have a panic attack, right there in front of *everyone*.

The last thing I wanted was for my future kingdom to think that I wasn't fit to be Queen, but honestly? Even *I* wasn't entirely sure that I was fit to be Queen.

"The show must go on, right?" Kane whispered to me. There was an encouraging look in his eyes. To say that he seemed cool, calm, and collected would have been an understatement; even though it felt like the world around us was in total shambles, he was still ready to proceed with this thing we needed to do. The look on his face told me there was no turning back now.

Maybe I really *had* chosen the right mate to be King.

We stood beneath the wooden arch that had been draped with sheer white fabric and featured dark pink garden roses and light pink peonies and waited for Professor Mindi Lee to begin speaking. Werewolves had to be married by a witch because there was a magical blessing portion of the ceremony to bind our souls together.

Milos's face flashed into my head then, and I knew why.

He was here and he was angry that I was marrying someone who wasn't him.

Fear filled my gut. My fight or flight instincts were in full swing, and all I wanted to do was run away. I would have, if it weren't for the fact that I was at my own wedding.

"Kane, Milos is here," I whispered to my mate.

As more shots rang out in the distance, Kane turned to Professor Lee. "Maybe it would be best if you skip to the important part, Mindi."

So much for all that time Maddie had spent bothering me about picking out the perfect vows. If only we had known at the time that we wouldn't have a use for them.

"Right," Mindi said with a nod. "Raven Gallagher, do you accept Kane Romero as your husband and your King, for all of eternity or until death do you part?"

Another knot twisted into my stomach, joining the rest of them.

Eternity was a *really* long time to promise to anyone... let alone to promise to one of your mates in front of the rest of your mates.

"I do," I said quietly.

"Kane Romero, do you accept the role as husband and King? Do you swear to protect Raven Gallagher and

JAYME MORSE & JODY MORSE

reign by her side for all of eternity or until death do you part?"

"I do," Kane said confidently.

"With the magic within me, I bind your souls together," Mindi said as she lifted her palms towards us.

Ribbons of neon blue light emanated from them, twisting around us and between us.

It looked so pretty.

I gasped as pain shot through me. It started in my chest before making its way down to my wrist.

I knew immediately that it meant my tattoo had changed again.

I held my wrist up to glance at it.

The Darken paw print now had cracks through it, giving it a shattered-looking effect.

At the very bottom of the paw print was a tiny black heart.

My heart started to pound as I glanced up into Kane's sparkling green eyes.

What if we had been wrong? What if this marriage wasn't *just* for show? What if it wasn't just the Darken tattoo that was shattered?

What if our wedding had changed everything between me and Rhys, Aiden, and Colton?

Were we shattered, just like my tattoo, for all of eternity?

CHAPTER 3

e hadn't even kissed.

All wedding ceremonies ended with a kiss, and yet ours had completely skipped that part, I realized, as Professor Lee stood off to the side so that our photographer could get a few photos of us.

I had always imagined my wedding to include a kiss at the end of our vows.

It was tradition.

I knew these photos would end up in paranormal history books. They would appear in all of the paranormal tabloids. And I didn't even bother to fake a smile for the camera. I was too shaken by everything that was happening: by the fact that I hadn't even kissed my husband, my mate, my King, and by the fact that there were still occasional gunshots being fired. They seemed to be getting further and further apart, which made me think that maybe Milos was running out of ammunition. At least, I hoped he was.

As our photographer directed us to stand in one final pose, Kane whispered, "You need to make a speech."

"What kind of speech? Maddie hadn't mentioned any post-vow speeches," I whispered back.

"Probably because Maddie didn't know that there was going to be a war on Nocturne Island during them," Kane said.

"Oh." *That* kind of speech. The kind that a Queen was supposed to make.

Except I wasn't a Queen yet. Not officially. Our coronation was supposed to happen the following week. Right now, we were just sort of in limbo. But I supposed that all of this was on me, considering it wasn't like we had anyone else ruling the werewolf kingdom.

That meant there was no one for me to take advice from, either. I was going to have to make my first speech without any guidance from anyone.

What if I did it the wrong way? What if one unprepared speech was enough to make the wolves hate me? What if, after this, they didn't want me to be their Queen?

I glanced over at Kane. "What do I say?"

Shaking his head at me in annoyance, he turned his attention towards our guests, leaving me staring at the side of his head, wondering why he was being like this.

"Thank you, everyone, for being here today," Kane said, his voice booming throughout the room. "In light of the events currently going on outside of these walls, we have decided to postpone our reception."

I hadn't expected that he would have been so good at speaking in front of a bunch of wolves he didn't know.

"As your future Queen and future King, we need your help. We are beginning a full search of Nocturne Island to find and eliminate our attackers," Kane went on. "Most importantly, we want to locate Milos Santorini. We will be outside waiting in the courtyard for you to join us in our search."

Kane grabbed my hand and started to lead me back down the aisle.

The wolves in attendance stood for us, but I couldn't help but notice that no one clapped.

There was always applause at the end of every wedding ceremony video that Maddie had made me watch while she planned mine.

I had this gut feeling that these wolves didn't like us.

AS WE REACHED THE COURTYARD, we found Aiden, Colton, and Rhys were already standing there, waiting for us.

All three of my matches were even more gorgeous than they normally did, if that was even possible. With their suits and ties, they all looked like they had just stepped out of a *GQ* magazine.

My mates looked so different from one another. It was like night and day between the three of them.

Rhys was the shortest of the three, and his auburn hair was slightly shorter than he normally kept it. There were no barbershops on the island, so my mates had been taking care of their own hair.

Colton was the tallest of the three. His blonde hair was

JAYME MORSE & JODY MORSE

on the longer side, and his skin was more sun-kissed than usual because of all the time we'd spent on the beach lately. He looked like he should have been a Lifeguard in California or something.

And then there was Aiden. His deeply tanned skin, and short dark brown hair set him apart from the others.

I knew that I had bigger things to worry about than how attractive they were. But even with the gunshots still occasionally being fired in the distance, all I could seem to think about was how drawn I was to the three of them.

As we walked towards them, though, I couldn't help but notice that none of them would even look at me. Colton's gray eyes were glued to the ground, and Rhys's dark blue eyes were darting around the courtyard.

As we approached them, Aiden's honey brown eyes completely avoided my gaze. Instead of looking at me, he glanced over at Kane.

I knew that all three of them were hurt because I had married Kane. For all I knew, they might have even been mad at me. And that fucking hurt. It wasn't like I had *wanted* to choose between the four of them. If it had been up to me, I wouldn't have chosen. But it was what I had to do in order to become Queen.

Kane had seemed like the most obvious choice because he was a part of the Triangle, but that wasn't the only reason I had chosen him.

It was *his* baby I was pregnant with. Not that he knew that yet. *None* of them knew it. It was a secret that I had been keeping, one that had been easy to hide until now because I hadn't begun to show yet. But I had noticed it this morning when I had put my wedding dress on: the slightest belly bulge. It wasn't a secret I would be able to keep for very much longer, and now that Milos had found a way to get onto the island, I knew that I was going to have to tell Kane.

"So, what's the plan?" Aiden asked.

"We're going to wait for everyone to show up, and then each of us will lead a group in different directions," Kane explained.

"Yeah... about that," Maddie said breathlessly as she came to stand with us, her mate and husband, Branden Mitchell, following after her. "I don't think anyone else is coming."

"What makes you say that?" I asked.

"Well, they all kind of walked in the opposite direction," Maddie told us.

"Like, towards the exit so they could get the hell away from us," Vince said with a shrug as he and his own mate, Julie, joined us.

"*Everyone?*" Kane asked.

Maddie and Vince nodded.

"Wow," I said, raising my eyebrows. "I can't believe that not even a single person stayed."

"Really?" Kane asked, shooting me another annoyed glance. "It makes plenty of sense to me. Their own Queen couldn't even ask them to stay. *I* had to ask them, and they don't even know who I am. Aside from the fact that I'm *your* husband, I'm completely unimportant to them."

"I'm not their Queen yet," I protested.

"You practically are."

"But it's not likely any of them know who I am. Not many of them, anyway."

JAYME MORSE & JODY MORSE

"They all know who you are," Kane argued. "They might not be close with you. Hell, they might not have even held a conversation with you before. But at the end of the day, you *are* still Princess Fallyn, whether you like it or not. That means that you have more sway over them than I do. You are royalty. You should have spoken up."

I narrowed my eyes at him. "You could have told me what to say."

Kane shrugged. "I shouldn't have to."

"Yes. You *should.* Your job as the future King is to support your Queen," Colton said, folding his arms across his chest and glaring at Kane.

I glanced over at the rest of my mates. Both Aiden and Rhys had cold expressions on their faces as they gazed at Kane. I was really relieved that it wasn't me, at least. They thought he was being kind of harsh, too.

Kane's face twisted into anger. "And Raven's job is to *always* know what to say."

"I don't think it's *your* job to know what Raven's job should be," Rhys said sharply. I glanced over at him, surprised. Out of all of my mates, Rhys had always been the sweetest and the most easygoing. I hadn't ever heard him snap at anyone like that before.

"Can we all just agree that we need to find Milos before he finds us?" I asked.

All of this was making my head spin.

I was right. This wedding really *had* changed us.

"Yes. Now what do we do?" Maddie asked. I could tell what she was doing; she was trying to shift the subject so that all of my mates would stop arguing.

"I don't know. Considering we have no help, I guess

we're going to have to search all on our own," Kane replied with a shrug.

"We should probably separate into groups," Aiden said. "Raven, you come with me. Colton and Rhys, you guys can go together. Maddie and Branden, you should both team up with your mates."

"I'm sorry, but my *wife* will be teaming up with me." Kane stared at Aiden through narrowed eyes.

"We don't have time for the two of you to argue right now. We need to keep you separated until you get your attitude under control," Aiden insisted. "We need to focus on finding Milos and whoever else Milos brought to Nocturne Island with him."

"You seem to be forgetting who the Alpha of this pack is," Kane snapped. "In case you need a reminder, it's not you. Raven will go with me."

"Actually, I think I want to go search with Aiden." I shot Kane an annoyed glance that should have told him not to question me.

"Doesn't being the future Queen mean more than being Alpha?" I heard Vince ask Maddie.

The truth was that I was upset about how he had snapped at me over the speech after the wedding ceremony. I really didn't want to be around him right now.

And honestly? It was beginning to make me wonder if I had made the wrong decision. Even though I had thought that Kane would make the best King out of all of my mates, I was beginning to wonder if one of the others could have been a better fit for not just the throne, but also a better fit for *me*.

"Fine. Whatever. I'm going to go start searching," Kane

muttered under his breath. "I'll take the north end of the island."

Once he was completely out of earshot, Aiden glanced over at me. "Raven, are you okay?"

"Yeah."

At least, I hoped I would be.

CHAPTER 4

*A*fter we walked all over the grounds of the castle and our section of Nocturne Island, my wedding dress was completely dirty and tattered at the bottom.

Not that it mattered.

No one, besides my closest friends and my mates, were going to see me wearing it again tonight, anyway, since we'd had to postpone our reception.

Were we ever even going to reschedule it?

It wasn't like it had been a real wedding—the kind of wedding that I had always pictured myself having. It was just a sham. A deception, so that we would follow the rules so that I could become Queen.

That was all. Even though I had been able to convince myself as I had walked down the aisle that it meant something, Kane's reaction to me made me realize just how wrong I was.

I supposed that, in a way, I had just chosen him because he was one part of the Triangle. That meant that along with Iris and Milos Santorini, who were the two other parts of the Triangle, he was one of the three most powerful werewolves and Alphas in the world. It had made him the most obvious choice for King, out of all of my mates. Kane being part of the Triangle meant that he had the ability to protect not just *me*, but the rest of my mates, too. Not that any of them would have ever agreed that they needed whatever protection Kane could offer to them.

But now I was beginning to have regrets. Had I chosen the wrong King? I was pretty sure that I had, but there was nothing I could do about it now. We were already married. The decision was already made. Our souls were already bound forever. Our marriage could never just end in divorce like a normal human couple could. The damage was already done. I was just going to have to deal with the fact that I had chosen a King who I was bound to butt heads with.

This was all about more than us, anyway. This was about all of the werewolves in existence. We had to make sure that this paranormal world war wasn't going to wipe out the entire werewolf population. So what if I had to sacrifice the idea of a happy marriage and the perfect husband? It was all for the greater good.

The vampires and witches were already deep into battles against one another, and a lot of the werewolf population was already being killed. And it had all happened because Milos and Iris had started those fires; it was all because they had started this war, for reasons I still didn't even understand.

I was pretty sure that it was just to torment me. Milos had told me in my mind that there was one way to end the war and that was to marry him. There was no way in hell I could marry such a monster. I was pretty sure this was all his way of blackmailing me into giving him what he wanted. He could have started a million wars, and I still wouldn't have married him.

Or maybe I was wrong. Maybe that wasn't even why he had started the war. Maybe it was for the power that came with it, or maybe it was because he and Iris were just downright evil. I could speculate as much as I wanted, but when it came down to it, I would never be sure.

The only thing I *did* know was that it was all about to end soon.

As soon as we found them on Nocturne Island, we would get rid of them, once and for all. Killing Milos Santorini was something that I had wanted to do for a long time now. I had been waiting years for the right moment—for Milos to slip up enough so that I could get to him.

For so long, I had thought that he'd murdered my parents. Even though I had learned that wasn't true, he had taken someone else who I loved with all of my soul, with all of my being.

Theo.

Because of Milos, Theo was gone, and he was never coming back. So, for that reason, I wanted to murder him more than I had ever wanted anything before. I wanted to avenge Theo's death, once and for all.

Then, once Milos and Iris were both gone, once I

became Queen, I would fix the damage they had done. I would declare that the war was over as soon as possible.

Since the werewolves were the ones who started it, thanks to Milos and Iris, we also needed to be the ones to end it.

"There's nothing out here," Aiden said quietly, snapping out of my thoughts.

I realized that we had passed the same tree more than once. "We haven't even heard any more gunshots. I wonder if maybe Milos left."

Aiden shook his head. "No. There's no way he left. He's just hiding. He doesn't want us to find him, for whatever reason."

"What do you think he was shooting at?" I asked.

Aiden shrugged. "I haven't figured that out yet. Maybe it was warning shots."

"Warning what, though? It doesn't make sense," I pointed out. "It almost seems like he was trying to make a big commotion to distract us."

"It makes sense to me. Milos probably thought all of the commotion would make you postpone the wedding." He pressed his lips together in a flat line. "But Kane made sure that didn't happen."

"Do you think I should have postponed it?" I asked as my stomach lurched.

I hadn't thought about getting the opinion of the rest of my mates because it was so sudden.

"I'll be honest. In the beginning, I thought that you shouldn't choose Kane. I thought that you should have chosen me, obviously. But that's just because of how I feel about you. I know that I could have given you the wedding you deserved… and I wouldn't have made you skip out on the vows that I would have written for you."

"But that's only because we were on a time limit. There was a threat and we had to get married fast," I pointed out.

He glanced over at me skeptically. "Is that really why? Why did he have to marry you so quickly? What difference would it have made if you had cancelled the wedding for even a few days?"

I considered it.

"He *was* the one who ultimately decided we should still get married, even though I thought there was a chance that we could get shot. My gut instincts were telling me to run," I admitted.

"I wish you would have," Aiden said softly. "But it's too late now. Now that you're stuck with him, we need to talk about how… different… he seems," Aiden said, his honey brown eyes sliding over to meet mine.

I knew that he wasn't wrong. Kane had always been so kind and caring towards me. Even though Theo had always told me he was a monster, I had never seen that side of him.

Not until *after* I had married him, that is.

"He's moodier," I agreed with a nod.

Aiden glanced over at me. "Is he moodier, or is he just letting you *see* his moody side now that you're married?"

My eyes widened.

I didn't want to admit that Aiden could have been right, but… it made sense that he could be.

"He's letting me see his moody side now that he no longer has to impress me. Now that I chose him to become my husband, he *knows* he's going to become King, either way. He doesn't have to keep trying to win me over anymore. Our souls are bound."

And, more than anything, I really wished that we could unbind them.

CHAPTER 5

*L*ater that night, my mates and friends and I all sat around the table in the castle's dining quarters, eating the food that should have been at our reception.

Even with my werewolf appetite, neither the grilled salmon nor the multiple shrimp dishes seemed the slightest bit appealing.

For the longest time, we all sat in silence. I knew that all of us were feeling the same way. We all felt defeated.

After searching every inch of the island, we hadn't been able to locate Milos or Iris. In fact, there were no signs they had even been on the island at all.

Gloria and the other witches were working on putting the veil back over the island, but I wasn't sure if it would even make a difference. It sort of just seemed like a waste of time. The two werewolves who we had really wanted to keep away more than anyone else were already here... *somewhere.* I'd had this feeling that the whole time we were searching for them, they had been watching us.

I couldn't shake the image of the two of them hiding in a tree or buried beneath the sand right near where we were walking from my head. There were so many ways that they could have hidden themselves from us, and each possibility made shivers creep their way down my spine.

"They're probably using an invisibility spell," Kane commented from where he sat at the head of the table, diagonal to me.

I supposed that he would know about invisibility spells better than any of us would. He'd had a lot more practice with them than any of the rest of us have had. The first time I remembered ever being under an invisibility spell myself was back during the ancient times, when I was Princess Fallyn and he had helped me escape from the castle and, more importantly, from the King and Queen.

"So, how do we make them un-invisible?" Maddie asked as she speared a bright red grape tomato, drizzled with balsamic vinaigrette, with her fork.

"Well, we could see if Gloria can come up with a spell to undo it," Kane explained.

"Perfect. There *has* to be a way. A spell. I bet if Gloria doesn't know of any, Professor Lee will probably know a spell we can use. I just know it," Maddie insisted.

Kane darted his eyes off to the side and I could tell it was to avoid rolling his eyes at her. I wondered if it was that he found her annoying, or pushy, or if he was just irritated that he hadn't thought of the idea first.

Either way, his reaction to my best friend had annoyed me.

"In the meantime," he went on, "we can just wait for them to decide to become visible again."

"That's it? We're just supposed to wait for them to become visible again? That sounds like the *worst* idea ever. Who knows where they might want to show themselves? Who knows how long it will take? We could be waiting forever. Maddie's idea is so much better. I say we do that one," I said firmly, crossing my arms over my chest.

Maddie flashed me a grin.

"Trust me when I say eventually you get tired of not being seen. I would know. I spent an entire year invisible."

Of course he had.

"When was that?" I asked, glancing over at him with raised eyebrows. I was surprised that Kane had never mentioned this before now. We had spent so much time together that I thought I knew *everything* about him; the fact that he still seemed to have secret parts of his life that I knew nothing about still amazed me. Then again, I supposed that must have been what happened when you had lived literally hundreds of years. There were so many years to cover.

"A while ago," Kane murmured, his emerald green eyes avoiding my gaze.

The way he refused to even look at me made me suspect the absolute worst of him. Why was he being so secretive of it? And *"a while ago"* wasn't even a good response. Anytime from a few months to hundreds and hundreds of years ago could have been considered *"a while ago."*

Ever since we had said *"I do,"* Kane had been revealing

that he was a lot sketchier than I had ever thought he was. He reminded me of an onion, peeling off each sketchy layer before all that was left of him was nothing that even resembled who he had portrayed himself to be. I knew that when all of the layers came off, there wasn't going to be anything likeable about him anymore.

And the worst part of that was that our souls were permanently bound together. I was going to be stuck with him for an eternity.

"And why did you go invisible for a whole year?" Aiden questioned.

"That's a really long time," Rhys commented.

"It must have been incredibly boring," Vince said.

I hadn't wanted to ask any further questions myself because I wasn't sure if I even wanted to know what he was doing while he was invisible for a whole year, let alone the reason why he went invisible for that long in the first place.

"Different reasons," Kane said with a shrug. "Different *problems*. It boiled down to going invisible for a year would help solve them."

"What type of problems could make you want to run away for an entire year?" Aiden narrowed his eyes at him.

"While invisible," Colton added.

I got the sense that they were just as suspicious of this whole thing as I was.

A glance around the table told me that almost everyone was leaning in closer, waiting expectantly to find out the answer.

"Oh. You know." Kane twisted some pasta around his fork. "A wife."

"A *wife?*" I asked, feeling my chest tighten. "You never mentioned that you were married before."

That was a very important detail that he should have told me about. His soul had been bound to someone else's before it was bound to mine. That was the absolute definition of getting some other girl's leftovers. Why hadn't he thought it was important enough to mention to me?

He kept twirling his pasta, completely avoiding my gaze. Then, he took a long, slow bite while everyone watched him.

He was *stalling.* He had felt at ease telling my mates and my friends all about his past, but he didn't want to have to *talk* to me about any of it?

Kane swallowed and smirked. "You never asked."

"I didn't think I had to!"

"Well. Yeah. I was married. Her name was Miriam." He shrugged.

"Aren't you still… together? Werewolf marriages are permanent," Maddie pointed out.

"Did you turn my best friend into a sister wife?" Vince asked accusingly. He looked annoyed by the idea.

"Werewolf marriages are for eternity or until death do you part. She died," he informed us with a nonchalant wave of his hand. "It's all good. Trust me, one wife at a time is *more* than enough."

He sounded so uncaring about the fact that his *wife* had died.

"Oh. So, you're a widower then. How tragic," Vince murmured. It was clear that he had noticed Kane's lack of emotion, too.

"So, you went invisible for a year because your wife died?" Aiden questioned.

"No. I went invisible for a year because they wanted to arrest me for her murder," Kane replied simply.

"That's horrible! You must have been so heartbroken." Vince commented. "Why would they think that about you?"

Kane shrugged. "I don't know. Maybe because I did."

A pin-dropping silence fell over the room as we stared at him with horrified looks on our faces.

Was he serious?

He couldn't have been serious...

And yet, the way that he had calmly gone back to eating his dinner told me that I had, without a doubt, married a monster.

CHAPTER 6

*A*fter we entered the tea room for dessert, my phone pinged with an incoming text message.

Glancing down at my phone, I saw that it was from Maddie.

Realizing that neither she nor Vince were in the tea room with us, I opened up the text message.

Maddie: S.O.S. Come to my room ASAP. Vince and I need to talk to you.

"I'll be back soon," I announced.

Kane's emerald green eyes locked on mine. "Where are you going?"

"I just need to help Maddie with something in her room," I lied.

The last thing I wanted was for him to know that my friends had to talk to me in private. I wasn't positive, but I was pretty sure that they wanted to talk to me about him… about what we had just learned.

"It's our wedding day. Can't it wait, whatever it is?" Kane asked.

"I don't think it will take long."

"Well, we're almost done here, so why don't you meet me in the King's Quarters once you're done?"

The truth was that I didn't want to be alone with him. Not after what I had learned tonight.

But instead of arguing about it, I simply nodded. Without saying another word to him, I headed out of the room.

I was about halfway down the hallway when I heard someone say, "Raven?"

Glancing over my shoulder, I found Aiden standing behind me.

I came to a stop, allowing him to catch up to me.

As he approached me, his honey brown eyes locked on mine. "Are you okay?"

"Honestly?" I took a deep breath. "I don't know. I don't think I am."

I knew that I didn't need to explain the reason was because I hadn't realized what I was getting into when I had married Kane. I hadn't known what a monster he was.

Of course, that was only *if* he had really killed Miriam.

But who was I kidding? My gut instincts told me that he really had. Why else would he have said it?

Aiden didn't ask me to elaborate on why I wasn't okay. He simply wrapped his arms around me in a strong embrace. His body was rock solid, and the truth was that I felt incredibly safe with him.

I knew that I would never feel safe like that with Kane again. Sure, he had never hurt me. In fact, he had done the opposite. He had killed Javier, my former professor and blood mate. Kane had done it to protect me... or so he had claimed. But now, I couldn't help but wonder if he secretly just had a secret desire to kill.

What if I truly was next?

"I won't let him hurt you, Raven," Aiden murmured into my ear. "I'll make sure that you're safe... always."

I knew that he meant every word.

I cried against his chest for a few moments, dampening the white shirt he wore under his suit, before finally breaking away from him. "I'm so sorry."

I'm so sorry for not choosing you or one of the others. That was what I really wanted to say, but I couldn't bring myself to admit that out loud. Admitting it would have meant admitting just how much I had fucked up... well, everything: my life, my future, all of eternity. No matter how I wanted to look at it, I had chosen the wrong guy.

"Don't be, Raven. I love you." He glanced over his shoulder to make sure that Kane was still in the tea room and then he brought his lips down on mine.

I kissed him back, wishing that everything was different. I wished that I could turn back time, for even just an hour—just long enough to not say "I do" to the wrong guy.

* * *

Vince opened the door to Maddie's room immediately when I knocked.

When I stepped inside the room, I noticed the grave looks on their faces.

It was obvious that they were both extremely worried about me.

"Are you okay, honey? That dinner was... intense." Vince shot a sympathetic look in my direction.

"I... I'm not sure what to think," I admitted quietly.

"Do you think he really killed his wife?" Maddie asked me, her chocolate brown eyes wide and full of concern.

My gut kept telling me that he had. There was the fact that you wouldn't just drop a bomb like that if it wasn't true. A part of me wanted to believe that he was joking, but he hadn't actually said that it was a joke. He hadn't said that it wasn't true, so therefore, I could only assume that it was.

But there was something else, too. It wouldn't have been the first time he had killed a girl. Aiden had once told me about a girl who Kane had murdered because she hadn't returned his interest. According to Aiden, that was what Kane did whenever he couldn't get his way with other wolves—especially wolves who were girls.

The only difference was that his *wife* had clearly been interested in him, so what was his reason for murdering her?

I glanced over at Maddie. "I think there's a pretty good chance that he did kill her," I replied with a nod.

"So, I guess the bigger question is, do you think he would kill you, too?" Vince asked me quietly. It was the elephant in the room, the question that had been swirling around inside my mind ever since I had found out about Miriam.

Up until now, I had only ever thought that Kane had nothing but love for me, but honestly? He was beginning to seem like a serial killer. And if he could murder both of those other girls, then who was to say he wouldn't he murder me, too?

If anything, he had more to gain from murdering me. If he killed me after we became King and Queen, then he would still remain the King of the wolves. Without me alive, he would become the sole leader of our kind. That obviously came with a good deal of power—more power than he would have as King to the blood-born Queen, the heiress to the werewolf throne. Without me around, he would have no one to answer to.

I didn't want to believe that Kane could have been capable of any of that.

But a sinking feeling that all of Kane's past lovers were in a graveyard filled my gut.

"I don't know," I admitted, answering Vince's question.

"I'm afraid for you," he admitted.

"I am, too," Maddie chimed in.

"Me, too." There was something else that was plaguing my mind, too. If he murdered me, he would also be murdering the baby that I was carrying.

Not that he knew that yet. I still needed to tell him about the pregnancy. Maybe if he knew, he wouldn't kill me. At least not until after the baby was born, anyway.

As far as I knew, Kane didn't have any other children. But that really didn't say much. How much did I really know about him, considering I hadn't even known before tonight that he had been married in the past? Maybe he did have some kids out there who he had never bothered to mention.

"I'm sure it will be okay, you guys," I said finally, even though I wasn't convinced of it myself. Not entirely, at least.

Kane had always seemed to care so much for me. I didn't want to accept that he would do anything to hurt me, but I had one thing in my favor, one thing that I believed would stop him in his tracks: *My other three mates.*

I knew that Aiden had meant it when he'd said he would keep me safe. Since he, Rhys, and Colton were my mates, that meant they could feel my emotions as if they were their own. If something were to happen between Kane and me, they would be able to feel that something was wrong. They would check on me to make sure that I was okay. And, if I had to guess, I was pretty sure that the three of them were already going to be on edge themselves after learning that Kane had killed his wife.

It was really lucky that Kane had felt so comfortable around all of us to share that news. My mates and my friends all got to experience it firsthand, versus me telling them about it. It probably caused it to have a bigger impact on them. I knew they were all going to be watching my back.

"Do you think it's even safe for you to spend the night with him?" Maddie asked me.

I realized what she was saying. It was our wedding night. We were supposed to spend it together.

Would he try to kill me that fast?

"I don't think he would do anything to hurt me tonight —not after he just admitted to everyone at dinner that he killed his first wife." Sure, Kane might have been crazy, but I didn't think he was stupid. He had to have known that if something happened to me tonight—or *ever*, really —all eyes would be on him. And I was pretty sure that if my other mates found out that he killed me, he would be dead so fast it wasn't even funny.

Except my other mates couldn't kill him, I realized. According to the prophecy about the Triangle, I was the only one in the entire world who was capable of killing him.

Was that another reason Kane would have wanted me dead? If he got rid of me, then he would have been completely invincible because no one else could kill him.

"I guess you have a point about that. He would look guilty as fuck. I just don't trust him with you," Vince said with a sigh. His hazel eyes met mine. "Promise us that if anything happens, you'll let us know?"

"I promise. You guys will get an S.O.S. text so fast, you won't even know what hit you."

"I'm more worried about Kane hitting *you*. Or worse," Maddie said.

"But I'm going to sleep with my phone right next to me and one eye open to make sure I don't miss any notifications," Vince quickly added.

"And we're just down the hallway," Maddie reminded me. "If anything happens, all you need to do is scream and we'll be there."

"Okay. I'll remember that. We should all be really careful right now, anyway," I said, glancing over at them.

45

"It makes me sort of nervous that both Iris and Milos are on this island somewhere. If Iris is going to hurt anyone, it's going to be one of us. We're the only ones she knows here. We're the only ones that she has any ties to. She'll probably come after me first, but I could see her doing something to hurt one of you guys, too."

"Oh, let her try." Vince shook his head angrily at the idea. "I fucking *dare* her to try to get past *my* mate."

"*Julie?*" Maddie let out a snort. "She's so sweet. That girl wouldn't hurt a fly."

"Oh, trust me. You have no idea. You haven't seen Julie when she's pissed off. When she's mad, she's not just a werewolf. She's like a rabid werewolf. She'll tear your fucking head off. If I was Iris, I would be afraid… *very* afraid."

"Let's just hope that Iris doesn't try anything," I said with a sigh. Our security guards were still out searching for both of them. So far, they apparently hadn't located either of them or I was sure that we would have heard something. But I just kept hoping that they would turn up at some point.

I hesitated for a moment at the doorway. "I need to get back to my husband."

"I still can't believe you're married," Maddie commented.

"To a *murderer*," Vince added quietly.

"Okay, aside from that part." Maddie tapped her chin thoughtfully. "Do you think he was kidding? Maybe he was just kidding. I *hope* that he was kidding."

"He wasn't kidding." Vince shook his head. "Did you

see the way he ate his lemon meringue pie afterwards, without a care in the world? He looked guilty as fuck."

"He definitely did it," I agreed with a nod. "But maybe he had a good reason for it."

"A good reason to murder his wife?" Maddie looked skeptical. "Is there *ever* a good reason to murder your wife?"

"I don't know. I want to believe that maybe she was some sort of monster." *Or more of a monster than he was, anyway.* A monster that deserved it.

But a voice at the back of my mind was telling me I was wrong.

"Well, why don't you ask him?" Vince asked.

"Tonight?" I just stared back at him, wide-eyed.

"I mean, now is as good a time as ever, isn't it?"

"Yeah, ask him while it's still relevant and fresh on both your minds," Maddie agreed with a nod.

"But it's our wedding night," I insisted.

Vince let out a snort.

Quickly jabbing him in the ribs, Maddie said, "It's true, though. Wedding night or not, if you're going to bring it up at all, now is the best time to do it."

Part of me didn't want to ruin our wedding night by asking Kane why he'd murdered his wife. What if he *did* have a valid reason? If he did, then maybe I could relax about all of this and we could move past this.

But I knew the real reason I didn't want to ask him— and that was because I didn't actually *want* to know the truth. I almost felt like the less I knew, the better, in a way. If I could postpone knowing why the guy I had chosen to marry—the guy whose baby I was also carrying—had murdered his last wife, the better off it would be for everyone.

There was one thought that just kept running through my mind, one that I couldn't seem to bury, no matter how badly I didn't want to think about it.

If Kane was as big of a monster as I thought he might have been, did that mean our baby was going to be a monster, too?

Even though I had always planned to tell Kane about the baby before anyone else, I suddenly had second thoughts about that. What if he found out and wasn't happy about the pregnancy? What if it made him want to kill us, too? I knew that was an extreme reaction, considering Kane had only ever made it seem like he wanted to spend the rest of his life with me. But it seemed like a good idea to let my friends know... *just in case.* At least then if I ended up dead immediately after telling Kane that I was pregnant, they would know why.

"You guys, there's something I need to tell you," I told my friends then. "But you have to keep it a secret for now. I don't want all of my mates to know just yet. Can you do that for me?"

"Of course," Maddie replied with a nod.

"Yeah. You know you can always trust us with anything," Vince added with a nod.

I could tell from the looks on their faces that they were worried that whatever I was going to say next was going to be on par with Kane murdering his wife. I realized that they thought that he was an even bigger monster than *I* thought he was.

I swallowed hard. "I'm pregnant."

"With whose baby?" Maddie's dark eyes grew really wide.

"Kane's," I replied quietly. "That's the reason I chose to marry him instead of the others. Well... *part* of the reason, anyway. It was a huge deciding factor."

"Wow. That makes so much sense now." Vince stared back at me sadly. "He's the last one that I would have thought you would choose."

Maddie nodded her agreement. "How far along are you?"

"So, officially... I don't know. Gloria told me that with Ancients, there's no way of actually knowing with werewolf pregnancies," I explained. "It's not the same as a traditional werewolf or human pregnancy. A lot of fate is involved, and you can stay pregnant for up to three years."

"Three years?" Vince's jaw dropped. "Ancient werewolves are closer to elephants when it comes to pregnancy."

"Elephants are only pregnant for almost two years, not three," Maddie said. "Why do Ancient pregnancies take so much longer?"

"Because we have a lot more magical abilities, and it takes longer for them to develop. Or it can take longer, that is. We can give birth as early as six months. That's why Gloria thinks it could happy any day now."

"So, technically, doesn't all of this mean that *any* of your mates could have gotten you pregnant?" Maddie asked casually.

I knew that she was probably hoping that it wasn't Kane's. I couldn't even say that I blamed her. If I could travel back in time and undo everything… well, I really wished that was possible.

"Well, we can rule out it being Rhys's," I replied. "I didn't do it with him until August, which was *after* I already knew I was pregnant. But I had sex with Kane in April for the first time, and that was the last time I had a period. So, I'm pretty sure I'm about six months pregnant." I paused for a moment and then turned. "I'm *just* starting to show right now, if you look closely enough, and I felt the baby kick during the ceremony."

I knew that it probably sounded crazy, but I couldn't help but wonder if it was some sort of warning now. Had my baby been trying to tell me that I shouldn't marry Kane? I couldn't help but feel like it was some sort of sign now that I knew about this deep dark secret from Kane's past.

"Well, congrats," Vince offered.

"Yeah, congratulations," Maddie said quietly. "I'm so excited to be an aunt."

"And me an uncle," he agreed with a nod.

But the looks on their faces told me that they were anything *but* excited for me. Their responses were forced.

I knew it wasn't that they weren't excited that I was about to become a mom. It was just that they were nervous and probably a little fearful about who had fathered my unborn child.

"So, you haven't told the rest of your mates yet?" Vince asked.

I shook my head. "No. And I'm not sure how they're going to take it, to be honest—especially now that we know he killed Miriam." Though, the truth was, what their reactions would be like was the least of my worries. I wasn't even sure how my now husband would take the news about our child. "Kane doesn't even know. I guess I'm going to tell him tonight." I paused for a moment before adding, "After we, uh, consummate the marriage."

"You're going to sleep with a murderer?" Maddie's dark eyes widened.

"I've already slept with him. Does it even make a difference now? I've *already* slept with a murderer."

"Yes," Vince said with a vigorous nod of his head. "It does make a difference now that we all know the truth."

I swallowed hard for a moment before adding, "Besides, we're already married. Murderer or not, we just permanently bound our souls together and agreed to be together for all of eternity."

"Well, there is one way out of that, you know," Vince said quietly.

"There *is?*" I hadn't had a chance to talk to Professor Lee or Gloria yet to find out if there was some sort of way to reverse our marriage bond. But as far as I had known, there was no way out of it.

"Yeah." Vince nodded, a serious look on his face. "We could always kill him."

CHAPTER 7

I headed towards the King's Quarters, which Kane had already been living in for over a month now. He moved in the day I had asked him to marry me, to be my King, and had stayed there while we were waiting for the wedding to approach. Traditionally, the King and Queen maintained separate bedroom quarters in paranormal society. I had been okay with that, because it meant that I could spend our off nights together with my other mates, either in the Queen's Quarters or in their own rooms.

As I walked to Kane's room that night, it wasn't the same. Normally, I walked to his room with a little pep in my step and butterflies swarming around inside my stomach. But this time, with every step I took in his direction, it felt different.

This time, I couldn't help but feel sick to my stomach.

So many thoughts were swarming around inside my head, but there was one thought that kept rising to the surface—no matter how hard I tried to push it to the back of my mind. And it was the scariest thought of all.

My best friends actually wanted to murder my husband— my mate—to prevent him from murdering me. The thought made my heart ache a little, because at the end of the day... he was still my mate. I did love him.

But the worst part about it all was that it may have been the best possible solution, depending on the reason he had murdered Miriam. It was a solution that I actually might have *liked*, even though I wanted no part in it.

I knew that it was all just hypothetical at this point. Who knew if it would ever actually lead to any of that? But if it did, it made me sad to think that my son or daughter would grow up without a father.

Then again, maybe my son or daughter would be better off without Kane. Did I really want him or her to grow up with a serial killer of a father? The last thing I wanted was for my baby to grow up to be a monster, too. Besides, I knew there were other strong male figures in my life who would be there for my child... and for me. I was thinking of the rest of the Darken and Vince. They would be there for both of us, whether we murdered Kane or not.

Correction: Whether *my friends* murdered Kane or not. Even though I knew that it seemed like a realistic solution, there was no way I could help them. They couldn't just ask a girl to murder her own mate.

Truthfully, the idea of living with him at all sounded horrible. I knew that losing him would hurt. In fact, I knew exactly how much it would hurt; it would feel the same way losing Theo had felt. But deep down, I knew

that it was something that might have needed to happen...
depending on the reason Kane had killed Miriam, that is.
If he had a good reason to murder her, then I knew we
could forget all of this.

Deep down, I had a feeling that he hadn't had a good
reason. If he had really killed the girl who Aiden had told
me about *and* Miriam, it meant that this was a pattern for
him. If he had killed two girls, he had probably killed
more, which meant two things:

1). He was probably a serial killer. I was not only
mated to and had married a serial killer, but I had chosen
a serial killer to become King; and

2). He was probably going to try to kill me next.

I wasn't sure how I had ended up in this mess, but I
couldn't help but want to blame Milos for all of it. Milos
had killed Theo, and it felt like everything in my life had
gone completely downhill ever since Theo had been
gone.

*If it weren't for Milos killing Theo, there was a good chance
I might have never married Kane at all.* Even though that
thought kept entering my mind, I knew that I couldn't
dwell on it. I knew all too well by now that you couldn't
change the past.

Then again, I was pretty convinced that you couldn't
change the future, either. I had already seen way too many
prophecies come true in this world to believe that making
different choices could really alter the outcome of what
would happen next. I was a firm believer in fate and destiny.

When I reached the King's Quarters, the door was
unlocked. I didn't even bother to knock.

As I entered the room, I found Kane laying in his bed. His back was turned to me, and he was watching *Paranormal House Hunters*, a reality show where mediums helped paranormal beings find houses that weren't haunted.

"Ahem," I cleared my throat from behind him.

Kane glanced over his shoulder and then a smile tugged at his lips. "Hey, my Queen. Have you come to consummate our marriage?"

I swallowed hard. We had talked about what our wedding night would be like for weeks now. He had promised that it would result in the most intense lovemaking session of my entire life.

But after tonight's turn of events, the truth was that was the absolute last thing I wanted to do with him right now.

At least, not until I found out the truth.

"Um, actually, I was thinking we could talk first."

"Oh, goodie." Kane flicked off the TV and then turned to me, giving me his undivided attention.

I stood there for a few long moments, unsure of what to say first.

"Are you going to come sit next to me?" He patted the bed next to him.

I hesitated. I wasn't sure how close I really should have gotten to him. Even though he had killed his last wife, he had always been incredibly sweet to me. He hadn't hurt done anything to hurt me in the past, but how could I really be so sure?

Reluctantly, I took a few steps closer to him and sat

down at the very edge of the bed, maintaining a safe distance.

"So, what is it you wanted to talk to me about?" Kane asked me, his green eyes locking on mine.

They were the same green eyes that had stared into mine as he had made love to me; the same green eyes that had told me he loved me so many times before. And they were the same green eyes that my baby had a chance of getting.

And yet, I felt like I no longer knew them. They belonged to a stranger.

"I need to know the reason why you killed Miriam," I said finally.

"Raven, I really don't want to do this right now." Kane shook his head.

Narrowing my eyes at him, I asked, "Why? Are you afraid that I won't be able to handle the truth?"

"No. I just don't want to ruin our wedding night," he explained. "It's supposed to be a good night. We shouldn't be talking about my past at all."

"You're the one who brought up how you killed your first wife. You practically bragged about it in front of everyone." I paused for a moment. "Wait, she *was* your first wife, right? Or were there others?"

He stared at me evenly. "She was my first and *only* wife before you." He sighed. "You're really going to make us have this conversation tonight, aren't you?"

"Yup." I nodded. "Because right now, you feel like a complete stranger to me."

"I've never lied to you, Raven. Everything I've ever told

you about me is the truth." There was a genuine look behind Kane's eyes.

"Yet, you somehow managed to omit the fact that you murdered your first wife until tonight," I pointed out.

"It's not the easiest thing to bring up," he said quietly.

"So, you did it in a room full of my closest friends and our pack. That makes perfect sense." The sarcasm was just dripping from my voice.

"What can I say? Liquid courage came over me. Plus, you were all questioning why I went invisible for an entire year. It kind of just popped out of my mouth before I really thought about what I was saying."

You mean before you could come up with a lie to cover up what had really happened. I couldn't help but think that was what he really meant. I wondered if he ever would have even told me if he hadn't gotten drunk or the whole conversation about invisibility hadn't come up.

I suppressed an eye roll. "Anyway, let's just cut straight to the chase. Why did you kill your wife?"

"Because," Kane said, meeting my eyes sharply, "she killed my mother."

"What? Why would she do that?" I choked out. I had been so certain, so convinced, that he hadn't had a good reason, that killing girls was just what he was. But there he was, handing me what may have actually been a valid reason to kill someone.

"My mother never liked Miriam. From the very first time they ever met, my mother thought she was… troubled." He paused for a moment, his mind seeming to drift back to the memories. "At one point, my mother even tried to convince me to end the marriage. She wrote me a letter pleading with me to break it off with Miriam. She didn't think it was a good idea for me to stay with her, given how toxic she was. She wanted me to find someone that would be better for me. She also expressed in the letter that she wanted me to find my mate. Miriam and I had gotten married, but it had always been a dream of mine to find you." His green eyes flicked over to meet mine.

I probably shouldn't have been getting butterflies in the middle of the story about why my husband had killed his last wife, but... there I was, feeling them swirling around inside my stomach.

"I had never been a Mama's Boy, or whatever you want to call it, but the truth is that she actually did convince me to leave Miriam at one point. I told her that we should separate from one another so we could both figure out if this marriage was what we even wanted or not."

"I thought werewolf marriages cannot be undone," I pointed out.

"A marriage bond doesn't permanently bond your souls together when you're not marrying your mate," he explained to me. "You can part ways at any given time. It's pretty much the same as a human marriage."

"Oh."

He paused. "Well, Miriam ended up finding the letter my mother had written me, and she just became full of so much anger and so much rage. She said that my mother was our enemy and that she wished my mother would just die. When I went over to my mom's house a few days later to visit, I found her dead body, and I just knew that Miriam was the one who had done it." His green eyes met mine. "I went into my own rage, I guess. I killed Miriam to avenge my mom's death. She deserved it. But I also did it because I didn't want to risk her hurting anyone else ever again."

"Trust me, I get it." I knew firsthand what it was like to want to avenge a parent's murder.

Now, I suddenly felt bad for thinking the worst of Kane—for thinking that *killing* him may have been my only option. Now that I knew the truth, I felt like we had more in common than I ever knew about. "I'm so sorry. I'm sorry you went through that, and I'm sorry that I felt suspicious of your intentions."

"It's okay, Raven. If you were the one who mentioned killing a former husband that I didn't even know about, I'm sure I would have had the same reaction."

"I just feel like I'm a shitty wife, and we've only been married for one day."

Kane leaned in closer to me and grabbed my hand. "You have nothing to apologize for. You are the furthest thing from shitty. It's me who should be apologizing. I'm sorry I snapped at you earlier about you not giving a speech. I guess I don't respond to high-stress situations as well as I thought I did."

"It's okay." I supposed that neither of us had been prepared for Milos to crash our wedding day. It was new territory for both of us. "But we need to learn to start communicating with each other better—and not just for ourselves, either."

"What do you mean?" His eyebrows shot up questioningly.

"There's something I need to tell you."

"I'm all ears." He leaned in closer to me, his green eyes not moving away from mine.

I took a deep breath. I wasn't sure why it was so hard to tell him this, even *after* learning the truth about why he had killed Miriam. There was nothing that should have made me doubt him anymore.

And yet, it took several long, awkward moments before I could force the words out of my mouth.

"I'm pregnant."

His green eyes widened. "With *our* baby?"

I nodded. "Yes."

"How do you know for sure that it's ours?" He studied my face.

I knew that it was a valid question. He knew that he wasn't my only mate who I had slept with. Still, I hated that it even needed to be a question. I hated that his first reaction was to imply that it wasn't his. Why couldn't he have just taken my word for it?

"You're the last one who I had sex with before I found out I was pregnant," I explained quietly. "I just... know."

"How long have you known?" Kane asked me.

"Since July," I admitted quietly. "I realized then that I hadn't gotten a period since before we did it in April."

"You found you were pregnant in *July*? It's September already." His green eyes met mine, and I couldn't help but think that he looked upset—or maybe even angry—that I hadn't told him before now. "You waited this long to tell me?"

"I'm sorry. I just needed time to process it on my own first," I explained. "This wasn't exactly how I saw my life going."

Well, technically, that wasn't true. It was exactly how I had seen my life going—*literally*. My mind flashed back to the vision that Gloria had shared with me, a vision that I was able to replay through my mind like a movie scene:

I was sitting on a throne at the Royal Palace on Nocturne Island. I was wearing a gold crown, which was adorned in sparkling sapphire and ruby gemstones.

The part that stood out to me the most was the bump.

I was pregnant.

My skin was glowing with radiance, and I looked so incredibly happy. I was pretty sure that it was the happiest I had ever seen myself.

"It is with great pride that I announce to you that the war has ended. While we mourn the deaths of the ones we have lost, we are relieved that more lives weren't taken from us. I promise you that, during my reign, we will never see a war as ugly as the one we are now free of."

At that moment, I watched as my mate walked across the stage. He, too, wore a crown, and people in the audience rose to him. That was when I knew.

He was more than just my mate.

He was my husband.

My King.

In that vision, I had seen that it would be him, that Kane was the one who I would end up choosing as King.

After I had seen that vision, I had planned to change the outcome of the vision. I had planned to change the future as a whole.

I was determined to choose Theo. Not just because of

Gloria's vision, but because he was the one who my heart was pulling me to the most. He was the one who felt right.

Well, it became clear that you couldn't just change the course of the future like that. Prophecies were real; there was no changing their outcomes.

Sometimes, I wonder if the entire reason Milos had murdered Theo just moments before I had planned to tell him that I was going to choose him was because my choosing him would have changed the way the future was supposed to play out. I didn't want to believe that Theo was meant to die, because I knew that he wasn't. Milos had taken his life from him prematurely. But it was if it was going to happen no matter what, which was why Gloria's vision had involved me choosing Kane.

After Theo had been killed, I felt like I had just given into her vision. I had accepted that this was who I was meant to be with. It may have sounded crazy, but I sometimes wondered if I would have chosen one of my other mates if I hadn't seen that vision. Even if I hadn't been pregnant, I was pretty sure that Kane was still the one who I would have ended up marrying.

If I hadn't known the plan that destiny seemed to have laid out for me, would I have made a different choice?

I would never know because I *had* seen it. So, I had chosen the mate who I had thought I would end the war with.

The good news?

The war would end before this baby was born.

The bad news?

A lot more lives were going to be lost before then. There would be a lot of destruction, a lot of tragedy, and a lot of heartbreak that would happen before the baby came into this world.

I could feel it deep in my gut.

Our lives were about to change even more than they already had.

CHAPTER 8

"So, does this baby... change... things?" I asked Kane as we laid in bed together that night. It was a question that had been circulating through my mind for months now, ever since I had found out that I was pregnant.

I knew this baby was bound to change something, and the truth was that I hated change. I wasn't sure if adapted to change badly, or if it was just that life had been throwing way too many changes my way lately.

He shifted onto one elbow and glanced over at me. "Like what?"

"The agreement." The Darken had agreed that I would continue to maintain relationships with all of them, even *after* Kane and I got married. While I had chosen Kane to be my husband, due to the close proximity to Theo's death, I hadn't felt like it was the right time to choose who I wanted to be with forever.

Deep down, I knew that logically, I would have no choice but to choose Kane in the end. He was my husband now, after all… and my King. Through our marriage, our souls were bound even more permanently than the mate bond. Even my tattoo knew that I was supposed to choose Kane.

I had heard about tattoos a werewolf got when they married their mate; they were permanent. Even *if* the mate died, the tattoo would last forever. That meant that the Darken paw print would always look shattered. Me and the rest of my mates would always be shattered.

That only left Kane.

But in order for Kane and I to move on in the way that he wanted us to, Gloria and Professor Lee would have to perform a spell to break my mate bond with my three other mates. Even though I knew that was something that was going to have to end up happening over time, the truth was that I didn't feel ready to give up the rest of the Darken. Not yet, anyway. My heart was still recovering from losing Theo; I really didn't think it was ready for me to break my bonds with the other Darken guys, too. My heart just couldn't handle it.

"Oh. The agreement." Kane paused for a moment. "You know that I don't *like* the agreement, right? I've never liked it. I've barely even had a say in it. This was something all of the Darken agreed to long before I ever came back."

I nodded. "I know."

"And the truth is that I like it even less now that you're my wife—my wife who's carrying my child." He paused for a moment. "But I know that we agreed that we wouldn't make any changes to your mate bonds until you're ready. So, I guess the baby doesn't change anything.

At least, not yet." His eyes met mine. "But after the baby is born, I think we should reevaluate the entire agreement."

"Okay. That seems fair enough," I agreed with a nod.

Truthfully? I wasn't exactly planning to jump any of the other guys' bones anytime soon. It wasn't fair to *any* of us, and honestly? I wasn't entirely sure how they would feel about that. I knew that they were all still bummed about the fact that I had chosen Kane to be King.

"I don't want to think about the other Darken, though. It's our wedding night, and right now, you're mine," Kane said, leaning in closer to me.

As his lips came crashing down on mine and we lost ourselves in one another, it felt like the two of us were the only ones in the entire world.

I allowed myself to forget about Miriam as he sent shivers cascading down my spine as he hit every nerve-ending in my body, driving me to the brink of ecstasy.

As we moaned and writhed together late into the night, I even almost forgot that I had three other mates.

Almost.

Because even as we exploded together, my heart still reminded me that all five of my mates held a piece of it.

"Raven? Wake up," Kane said, stirring me awake.

My eyes fluttered open, and I took in my surroundings. I was still laying in Kane's bed. I must have drifted off to sleep almost as soon as my head had hit the pillow.

Glancing at the clock on the nightstand, I realized that it was 4 a.m.

"Is everything okay? Is Milos here? Are Aiden, Colton, and Rhys okay?" My biggest fears flew out of my mouth before I could do anything to stop them.

"They're fine," Kane replied with a sigh. I could tell that I had really annoyed him, but he was letting it go this time because I was still half asleep. "Milos isn't here. But we need to get ready," Kane explained.

I frowned, sitting up in bed. "Ready for what?"

"The coronation. Gloria just called me. She had a vision. We need to become King and Queen sooner than we originally thought," he explained. "We can no longer do this ceremony in public. It's going to be a small, intimate affair with the ones we know we can trust."

I frowned. "I'm confused. Gloria was the one who thought we needed to make this a huge public spectacle. Now she thinks we need to make it small and intimate? I don't get why she's had such a drastic change of heart. Did she see something bad in her vision?"

She had to have.

"I'm assume that she must have." Kane shrugged. "I'm not sure what, exactly. All I do know is we need to get down to the cathedral as soon as possible to become King and Queen. We need to do it right away."

"Okay. I have to go back to my room to get my dress —" I started to say, but Kane interrupted me.

"I already went there after she called me," he explained. "Your dress is hanging in the bathroom."

"Okay." I climbed out of his bed and headed for the bathroom.

Once I was inside, I closed the door behind me and then pulled on the burgundy dress, which had a gold floral print on it. The dress was made of velvet and fell to my feet. It was just as soft inside as it was out.

Sure enough, Kane had also grabbed the gold heels I had picked out to wear with it.

This dress was something that Maddie and I had carefully chosen, knowing that it would end up in the tabloids and paranormal history books. It was disappointing that it wouldn't now.

Speaking of Maddie, I wanted her to be at the coronation.

"I want to wake Vince and Maddie up," I started to tell Kane once I had re-entered the bedroom. "I want her to witness this. She's been looking forward to it." Probably even more than I was.

I knew I probably seemed a little bit dramatic to him, but let's be real. Even he should have understood that it wasn't every day your best friend became Queen of the wolves. I would have wanted to be woken up if our roles were reversed.

"Already done," Kane said with a nod.

"Really? You thought to include them?" I just stared back at him in awe, surprised at how thoughtful he was.

"Gloria mentioned that we were going to need two witnesses, and I thought who better to include than your best friends? They're going to meet us down at the cathedral in fifteen minutes."

"Okay." I took a deep breath. A part of me felt like maybe we should invite the rest of the Darken. It was hard to envision myself becoming Queen without Colton, Rhys, and Aiden there to watch it happen. Every ounce of my being wanted them there, but honestly?

I wasn't sure if it was the best idea. Their hearts had already had to endure watching me marry Kane yesterday. Would they be able to handle watching the two of us become King and Queen, too? I didn't want it to be too much on them.

Even though I wanted to invite them, I figured that it was a better idea to just let them sleep through it. It had worked out perfectly, in a way. All of this was happening so last minute that I had a valid reason to not invite them.

It just made me sad that I was becoming Queen without all of them by my side.

Trying to push the other Darken guys out of my mind, I tried to focus on the right here and right now.

The moment that I had been waiting to happen for months now was finally happening.

Suddenly, everything about this felt so… rushed. I had known for months now that I was going to become Queen of the wolves, but it suddenly felt like everything was happening so fast. *Too* fast.

It felt like Kane was whisking me off in the middle of the night to become Queen. I barely had a chance to mentally process any of this.

"Ugh, my hair," I said, glancing at myself in the mirror. I ran a brush through it, trying to make the curls that were still in my hair from the wedding ceremony look a bit more controlled. But you could still tell that I had slept on them.

"Your hair," Kane said, moving to stand in front of me, "looks beautiful." I knew he was just trying to appease me so that I would hurry up. "You look absolutely stunning, Raven. My Queen."

"Your *Almost* Queen," I reminded him with a giggle. "We're not royals *yet.*"

"We're about to become King and Queen in a few short moments, my love," Kane said. "And to be honest with you, I've never been more excited in my life."

"Really? Not even when you married me?" I asked him through narrowed eyes.

"Well, yes. Of course. But now that that's in the past, this is the newest thing for me to be excited about." His green eyes locked on mine. "This is our first step as husband and wife. I love you, Raven."

"I love you, too." I smiled up at him.

"We'd better get going," Kane said as he pulled on his tuxedo jacket. "The last thing we want is to be late to our own coronation ceremony."

Well, it might have helped if the ceremony wasn't being held at 4 o'clock in the freaking morning, I thought bitterly. To say that I wasn't a morning person would have been an understatement. I loathed mornings. Especially right now, when I was about to become Queen when it wasn't even daylight outside yet.

I knew that far crazier things had happened.

And I was sure that it was all for a good reason. Gloria's visions were on point. My proof of that was the baby I was currently carrying.

When we got downstairs, we found that Maddie and Vince were waiting in front of the cathedral room for us. Vince was wearing a suit, and Maddie was wearing a short navy blue dress.

"Thank you guys for coming," I told them as we approached.

"This is all so abrupt. I'm sorry I'm such a mess," Maddie apologized, gesturing to her minimal makeup and somewhat messy wavy hair, but the way she was eyeing me told me that she thought I looked like a mess, too.

"You look great," I said, noting that she was wearing the navy blue velvet gown that we had picked out together.

"You really do," Vince said with a nod. "Both of you do. And of course we'll be here for you no matter what, Raven —rain or shine, daytime or at the butt crack of dawn," Vince added.

"You guys are great." Kane smiled at them. "Luke, the head of the Paranormal High Council, is meeting us. He'll be performing the ceremony. I'll go see if he's here yet." He entered the cathedral, leaving the three of us standing outside.

"Okay, so, did you find out the dirt?" Vince asked me once Kane was out of earshot.

"The dirt?" My eyebrows lifted.

"Yeah, you know." Maddie leaned in closer to me and whispered, "The reason why he killed his wife."

"If it's awful we can get you out of here," Vince added in a low voice.

"Oh. He had a completely good reason." I waved my hand at them. "I'm not worried about him anymore. I can assure you that he's not planning to kill me."

"Well, thank heavens for that," Vince said with a smile.

Maddie widened her eyes at him. "Did you really just thank the heavens?"

"If the shoe fits." He shrugged. "The last thing we want is to have to worry about our best friend being murdered by her husband, the King. That would be like a fairytale meets *Lifetime* movie."

I laughed. All I could really seem to think, though, was that my life was the furthest thing from a fairytale. I was about to become Queen, simply because I needed to end the war that was going on all around us. Though I supposed that life *did* feel a lot like a *Lifetime* movie sometimes.

"Really, though. Why did this have to happen at such an odd hour of the day? I've never even heard of a coronation taking place at 4 o'clock in the morning," Maddie said.

"*Not* that she's been to many coronations," Vince added.

"Kane told me that Gloria had some type of vision. She insisted that we become King and Queen as soon as possible."

"Was it a bad vision?" Maddie asked, her eyes full of concern.

"It seems bad. Like drag your besties out of bed as soon as possible bad," Vince said.

I shrugged. "I really don't know. Sorry. I appreciate that you guys were able to get up to witness it," I told them. "I really wanted to share this with you."

"What about the rest of your mates?" Maddie asked, glancing pointedly around us. "Where are they?"

"I didn't want to wake them up," I replied with a shrug. "They don't really do mornings well."

That part *was* true, at least. Aiden, especially, was like a bear when it came to getting up early in the morning.

Vince shot me a skeptical glance. "I'm sure they do mornings a lot better than Maddie."

"Hey!" Maddie gave him a glare. "But that's kind of true. And, I don't know, Raven, I just thought you would have wanted them here."

Before I had time to say anything else, Kane walked back into the room.

"Luke is here. We're ready." He took my hand and led me down the aisle—the same aisle I had walked down earlier that day to say "I do." It was the same aisle where I had felt so threatened by Milos. Walking back down the aisle sort of gave me PTSD, to be honest, but having Kane there by my side made everything so much better.

It was so relieving to know that I was going to have him by my side from here on out. We were in this together.

As we reached the front of the room, we stood before Luke, a short man. Judging by his frame, it was easy to see that he wasn't a werewolf, but I wasn't sure what type of paranormal being he actually was.

"This ceremony is a lot different than I was expecting it to be. I was surprised that you called me in the middle of the night," Luke told Kane.

"Yes, well, Gloria insisted that we do this as soon as possible," Kane replied.

"Well, we can't doubt Gloria, now can we?" Luke asked with a little laugh. "Since there are no spectators like we originally planned and this won't be televised, I guess we can skip straight to the oath."

"The oath?" My eyebrows lifted. I didn't have any idea

on what to expect with any of this. I hadn't known anything about coronation ceremonies.

Luke nodded. "I'll begin with you. Do you, Raven Romero, solemnly swear to protect the kingdom of the wolves for the duration of your reign as Queen?"

"I solemnly swear," I replied with a nod.

"And do you, Kane Romero, solemnly swear to protect the kingdom of the wolves for the duration of your reign as King?"

"I solemnly swear," my mate replied from where he stood next to me.

"Then, with the powers vested in me by the Paranormal High Council, I hereby dub thee Queen and King."

I glanced over at my mate. It was official. We were royals now.

CHAPTER 9

$\mathcal{L}$uke grabbed a crown from the podium behind him. "This crown once belonged to Queen Lydia, who I had the grand honor of knowing." He shot me a sympathetic glance. "I am terribly sorry for your loss."

"Thank you." I forced a smile as he placed the crown, which was gold and adorned in sapphires and rubies, on top of my head. The truth was that I was actually *relieved* that my biological mother was dead. From all of my memories, my mother—Queen Lydia—had treated me horribly. I was sure that there were probably a lot of horrible things that were still repressed, too.

All I did know was that, once my son or daughter was born, I would be a better mother than Lydia *ever* was.

"I have high hopes that you will be as delightful of a Queen as she was," Luke said.

I forced another smile.

I wondered what my mother's reaction would have

been if she could have known that I was standing here, married to the guy who had helped me escape from the marriage she had tried to force upon me. Kane might not have been the perfect husband, but I did know that I was a lot happier with him than I would have been with Milos Santorini, if my mother had been able to get her way. If only she could have known that I'd had no choice *but* to marry Kane, to take my rightful place as Queen, to stop the paranormal world war that had been started by the husband that she would have chosen for me. Mothers didn't always know best. Especially not *my* mother.

Walking over to Kane, Luke placed a crown on his head. "This crown was custom-made for you."

For some reason, it surprised me. Why did *he* get to have a brand new crown of his own while *I* had to wear my mother's? Maybe I was being dramatic, but it felt like hers had been tainted. And Kane wouldn't have even become King if it weren't for me. I deserved a new crown more than he did.

"Now, I need all four of you to sign the Royal Doctrine," Luke explained, snapping me out of my thoughts. "Once you have signed, you may retire back to your quarters."

"We'll be meeting Gloria after this," Kane said, shooting an emerald green-eyed glance, which matched the emeralds on his crown, in my direction.

Luke handed the pen to me first. I wrote *Raven Gallagher Romero* on the line. It felt so weird signing with my new married name for the first time ever. To top it off, I was pretty sure this was the most important thing I would ever sign in my life. The worst part about it was that his last name felt like it still belonged to him. It didn't feel like me at all. It felt like only half of my signature was mine.

As Kane wrote his signature on the line, Colton loudly asked, "Am I too late?"

Luke gazed over in his direction. "Too late for what, Sir?"

Colton hurried his way down the aisle. "Did the coronation already take place?"

Kane turned to him with a smile. "Yeah, it did, buddy. What's up?"

A defeated look filled Colton's eyes. He glanced over at me. "I need to talk to you."

"I'm sure that anything you have to say to Raven, you can say in front of me, too," Kane replied.

"What is it, Colton?" I asked.

"It can wait now," Colton muttered. "What you're doing is more important."

"No. What is it?"

His gray eyes met mine. "Can we talk in the hallway?"

Kane shot a glance in my direction, but I ignored it and followed Colton out of the room. "What is it?"

His gray eyes met mine. "Kane isn't who you think he is."

"Oh. If you're talking about what happened at dinner, it's okay. He told me the real reason he killed Miriam and —" I started to say, but Colton interrupted me.

"This has nothing to do with Miriam. It has to do with all of us." His eyes didn't move from mine. "Kane has horrible plans for once he becomes King."

"What do you mean by 'horrible plans'?" I asked him with raised eyebrows.

"He's not planning to *stop* the war. He wants to make it worse. He wants all of the paranormal beings to have to fight." His eyes met mine. "His end goal is for the werewolves to be the only paranormal race left.

CHAPTER 10

I just stared back at Colton for the longest time, trying to absorb everything he had just said.

Kane wanted to become King to wipe off other paranormal races.

He had woken me up and rushed me into this coronation ceremony in the middle of the night because he couldn't wait a second later to become King and intensify this war.

Kane wasn't good. That was the best way to sum it all up.

Was it possible that any of that was actually true?

When I glanced back into the room at Kane, I found his green eyes looking in our direction.

I was pretty sure that he was nervous about what Colton had just told me—clearly for damn good reason. Kane had secrets he obviously didn't want me finding out about. Until tonight, Miriam had been a secret. What other secrets could he have been keeping from me?

There was something else that I noticed, too. Ever

since Luke had placed that crown on Kane's head, he suddenly exuded power. It was this energy that just seemed to float in the air around him, even from how far away I stood. And suddenly, I just got this feeling that he *craved* it. He played the part well. He looked like a person who had been King his entire life instead of a few minutes.

I turned back to Colton. "How do you even *know* any of this?"

"Gloria just had a vision. She saw everything. She saw that Kane might try to force you to do the coronation earlier than we planned."

I rolled my eyes at this so-called evidence of how 'bad' Kane was. I was beginning to doubt everything he had just told me. "Yeah. Of course we're doing the coronation earlier. She *told us* to."

"Is that what he told you?" Colton asked, his eyebrows shooting up questioningly.

I nodded. "He said that Gloria saw something and that we had to do this now."

Colton let out a laugh, shaking his head. "And you didn't even think to question Gloria yourself? You just blindly took Kane's word for it?"

"I was half asleep. And what would have made me think that my mate... my *husband*... would lie to me about something like that? How do we know that Gloria isn't the one who's actually lying?"

"Two reasons. First of all, Kane has a bigger motive to lie than Gloria does. What does she have to gain from lying?" Colton asked.

"I guess," I replied, considering it. The truth was that it

wouldn't have been the first time the witch had lied to me. She had also pretended that I was meant to be in the Crescents' House back during the Sorting Ceremony at Werewolf Academy. The Crescents' House was for the "bad werewolves." I had spent the first three years of my time at Werewolf Academy actually believing that I was half-bad werewolf. At the end of the year carnival last year, Gloria had confessed to me that she had lied about it.

But the thing was, Gloria had only lied about it to help me. She had wanted me to learn how to protect myself from dark magic and bad werewolves because she knew that in the future, I would be faced with them.

I doubted that someone who had lied for so long in order to help me learn how to defend myself would lie to hurt me now.

Still, I wasn't entirely convinced that Kane had lied about Gloria's vision being the reason we had to do this coronation ceremony ASAP.

Or maybe it was just that I didn't want to believe that he had lied. That would have meant that I was in love with a liar, and that was the absolute last thing I wanted.

"So, what's the second reason?" I asked Colton.

"Well, here's the thing. There was a second part of her vision that has already ended up coming true," he explained.

"And what was that?" I pressed.

"That Iris and Milos are close. And she's right. They've been spotted."

"By who?" I asked.

"The security guards."

Goosebumps erupted all over my arms. "Where are they?"

"There's reason to believe they might have gotten into the castle."

"What? How?!" Panic raced through my veins.

"Someone let them in."

"Who?" I was beginning to feel sick to my stomach. Who the hell would have let those monsters into the castle? It looked like my first order of business as Queen was going to be to take care of this traitor, whoever it was.

"We're not sure," Colton replied, shaking his head.

"If they're inside the castle, then why the hell isn't anyone looking for them?" As the words left my mouth, I wondered if it was okay for Queens to swear.

Well, the truth was that I didn't give a shit. This Queen did. This was a swearing sort of situation.

"Rhys and Aiden are looking for them. That's the whole reason they're not here."

"Ugh. This is just freaking lovely. The first thing I want to deal with after becoming Queen at not even five o'clock in the freaking morning is Milos and Iris." The truth was that I wanted nothing more than to murder Milos, but I wanted it to be on my time and not when they were in the middle of ambushing us. "Should we hide? *I* should hide, right?"

Oh, god. So much for trying to act like I was this strong Queen. My words and my current urge to hide from Milos, from the guy who I had been preparing to kill for the past three and half years to kill, proved otherwise.

I was weak as fuck. It was almost laughable.

What was I even doing? How had I let Gloria convince me that this had even needed to happen in the first place? I clearly wasn't fit to be Queen.

"Relax, Raven," Colton said, his eyes meeting mine. Something about his gray gaze made me feel slightly more relaxed. "They were spotted in the dungeon at the east side of the castle. They're not going to get over here any time soon *or* that easily. The guards will catch them by then."

I let out a slight sigh of relief. I hoped he was right.

"Colton, why didn't you get here sooner?" I groaned. I knew it wasn't his fault, but still.

Colton's gray eyes turned stony. "Hmm. Why didn't I get here sooner to stop the coronation that I wasn't invited to and didn't even *know* was taking place? I tried to find you in the Queen's quarters and when it became evident that you weren't sleeping there, I figured I would try here in case Kane was rushing you to become Queen as soon as possible and, lo and behold, I was right. The real question is why did you choose *him*?"

"I just did what I thought was right for everyone—for all of us and the entire werewolf race," I explained.

"You really thought that *he* was the right thing?" Colton asked.

"He's one part of the Triangle, Colton."

"Even *more* reason to not choose him."

"That's one way to look at it," I replied, "but I chose to look at it the other way. He's a lot more powerful than the rest of us—all *four* of us, me included. He can protect us in a way that no one else can."

"Or destroy us," Colton muttered under his breath. "He's already done that."

My eyes flicked over to meet his, my heart breaking a little at his words. Was he saying what I *thought* he was saying? "What do you mean?"

"The dynamic of our pack has completely changed, Raven."

That right there was exactly what I was afraid of happening. I touched the tattoo on my wrist gently.

"It makes no sense, Raven. You've known the three of us so much longer than you knew him. He was still practically a stranger when you chose him. You didn't have to choose me, but you didn't have to choose *him*. None of us understand it. None of us understand why you've made such a mess of things."

He looked so disgusted with me. He looked like he wanted to be far away from me and the *mess* I made.

I stared back at him, my throat closing in on me.

"I need to go find the others, and we all need to go find Milos and Iris." Colton shook his head angrily at me before turning on his heel and sauntering off.

My heart pounded against my chest. Milos had already taken away one of my mates; I couldn't risk him taking Colton away from me, too—not when we were fighting this way. I wasn't sure what was going to happen when, or if, we found Milos and Iris, but I was pretty sure that it wouldn't be pretty.

"Colton, wait!" I called after him, but he didn't even turn to look in my direction. He just continued to walk slowly away from me.

Tears trickled down my cheeks as more welled up in

my eyes.

I felt a hand rub my shoulder reassuringly and glanced over to find Maddie standing beside me.

I wasn't sure how much of it she had witnessed, but I supposed that it saved me from having to tell her about it later.

"I just need a minute," I told her. "I'll be back in there in a minute."

"Okay." She nodded, pressing her lips together and heading back into the cathedral room where Kane was deep in conversation with Luke and Vince.

Leaning against the door, I tried to compose myself.

I had chosen the wrong King. The wrong husband.

All three of my other mates were mad at me.

To say that I had ruined everything would have been an understatement.

I had completely fucked everything up.

Tears stung at my eyes, and I tried to blink them away. It felt like the entire castle was closing in on me.

"How *did* you even make this all into a bigger mess than we did?" a familiar voice asked from behind me.

Turning around slowly, I found Iris standing there. Her short, strawberry blonde hair was a mess. It looked like she had been living in the wilderness for days.

"I'm sorry I missed your coronation, by the way. I would have *loved* to watch you become Queen. After all, doesn't everyone love to root for the underdog?"

As a wave of anger washed over me, I opened my mouth to say something, but no words seemed to come out.

Iris smirked. "Cat got your tongue, Queen?"

CHAPTER 11

"Queen Raven doesn't even *sound* good." Iris wrinkled her nose. "Dare I suggest you go back to Fallyn?"

"What are you doing here, Iris?" I finally managed to ask.

"What do you mean? Wasn't I invited for your big moment? I was your best friend, after all. In fact, come to think of it, we even shared a few intimate moments." She winked at me as she took a few steps closer to me.

I took one step back. I would have taken more, but my feet just felt rooted to the ground.

I felt sick to my stomach. I knew that she was referring to the time she had kissed me when Milos had kept me as a prisoner in his dungeon.

To enact the power that the Triangle was capable of, all three parts of the Triangle had to kiss me. It was all a part of the prophecy. Milos and Iris had been the first two to kiss me. It wasn't until I kissed Kane that the Triangle's powers had been fully ignited.

But thinking about those dark, horrible moments in the dungeon only made me feel a lot of anger and resentment.

"Okay, confession," Iris announced then. "I may have lied. I didn't just come here to watch you become Queen."

"Then what did you come here for?" I asked her.

"Oh, come on, Raven. Don't play dumb." Iris pulled a gun out of her pocket and pointed it at me.

My heart pounded against my chest. "Iris, please don't do this."

"Give me one good reason not to." She tucked a piece of strawberry blonde hair behind her ear.

"I'm pregnant," I informed her.

"So, you mean by killing you, I'd be killing you *and* your future spawn? Sweet." Amusement swirled around inside her eyes.

Who *was* this monster?

"It looks like you're going to have the shortest reign in the history of all paranormal Queens," Iris said with a grin. As she lifted the gun a little higher, she asked, "Any final words?"

I opened my mouth to speak again, but no words came out.

At that moment, I heard the sound of the gun being fired.

At first, I thought that Iris had shot the gun she was holding, but instead, *she* was the one who had fallen to the ground.

I glanced over my shoulder to find Maddie standing there, a gun in her hands.

"You just happened to bring a gun with you?" I asked with wide eyes.

"With this psycho and Milos on the loose, yeah. I've been carrying a gun with me just to pee at night," Maddie replied with a nod.

"Me, too," Vince said as he stepped out into the hallway, wrapping me into a huge bear hug. "I'm so glad you're okay."

I breathed a huge sigh of relief. My best friends were really freaking brilliant. "You saved my life."

"I know." She ran over to me and gave me a loose hug. "Now we just need to find and kill Milos."

I had a feeling that Milos was going to be a lot harder to find. He wasn't going to just show himself to us the way Iris had. Iris could never just resist the chance to taunt me.

At that moment, I heard laughter from behind us.

I glanced over my shoulder to find that Iris had sat up. "You girls are so silly. You really thought a *gun* could kill *me?* I'm part of the Triangle. We're far more powerful than silver bullets."

Shit. I had completely forgotten that important fact.

There was just one problem. I didn't actually know how you *did* kill the Triangle. Had it ever been in any of the history books I'd read about it? I tried to rack my brain to remember, but I couldn't seem to.

I wished that Aiden was here. He was one of the only ones who I could think of who might have actually had some idea of how to kill them.

Fuck.

We were here against Iris, completely defenseless.

Clearly, a silver bullet was enough to temporarily stun her, but that was it. I had no idea what else we could have done to stop this monster.

As she stared at me from across the hallway, all I could seem to think about was how invincible she was. And that scared the everloving crap out of me.

At that moment, I heard the sound of Iris's gun firing. *Fuck.*

Holding my breath, I watched as the bullet hit the stone wall above me before ricocheting off.

I exhaled and inhaled deeply, relieved that no one had been hit. It would take a silver bullet straight to the heart to kill us, and Iris didn't seem to have good aim.

As if on cue, she let out a wicked laugh. "I got you guys. I got you good." A look of seriousness came over her face then. "I think that I should aim for real next time. But who should die first?" Iris asked as she pointed the gun at Maddie, then Vince, then me. As she aimed it towards the ceiling, she said, "Decisions, decisions."

Maddie, Vince, and I exchanged a nervous glance.

I could hear my heart pounding in my ears. *Was she really going to shoot us?*

I knew that we probably should have ran, but my feet didn't seem to want to move. We weren't fast enough to outrun a bullet, either way.

Where the hell was Kane? It seemed like he had just disappeared, but why? He was supposed to be my King, my protector. Now that we were in a life-or-death situation, he had suddenly gone M.I.A.

"I know who I'll kill first," Iris announced then. "Maddie. I've never liked you, but you already knew that."

"Iris, please. We'll do whatever you want, but put the gun down," Vince pleaded with her.

"Oh, Vince. You were always the one to butt into everyone's business. Maybe, for that reason, I'll kill *you* first." She waved the gun in the air and then pointed it at him.

As she pulled the trigger, I whispered, "Friozo," the witch word for *freeze.*

I watched in awe as the bullet was shot out of the gun and then came to a stop. It lingered in the air. A few moments later, it fell to the ground.

Iris turned to me, her nostrils flaring with anger. "Really, Raven? You think you're going to get out of this using your magic?"

"Try me," I challenged, realizing that we wanted her to use all of her bullets. It was the best thing we could make her do. Once she ran out of ammunition, she couldn't hurt us.

At least, I hoped.

I wasn't sure what else she had up her sleeve to try to kill us with. I didn't know what sort of magic she was capable of since she was part of the Triangle. Though, if she was capable of using other methods to kill us, why had she chosen to use the gun? She had never been the best shot. Then again, she hadn't been that great with Lunar Magic either when we were back at Werewolf Academy, but that was *before.* Before the Triangle had officially been ignited.

I had to figure out a way to get rid of her.

Pointing the gun straight at my chest, Iris pulled the trigger.

"Friozo," I said, watching as the bullet fell to the floor.

But then something else happened, too.

A strong gust of wind filled the hallway we were standing in, and then Iris became covered with ice.

"Oh my god," Vince commented. "I'm pretty sure you just froze Iris."

I stared back at her. She was completely frozen in place, inside a human-sized ice cube.

"Can we keep her this way forever?" Vince asked.

"She might melt," Maddie pointed out.

"Oh, boo. I didn't think of that. I just thought it would have been the perfect punishment for everything she put us through," Vince said.

At that moment, the Darken and Gloria appeared in the hallway.

Colton hurried over to me and wrapped me in his arms, pulling me against his chest in the biggest bear hug. "I'm so sorry I left you."

"It's okay. I'm surprised you didn't hear the gunshots," I commented, unable to hide my annoyance at the fact that he hadn't been here during it. But I was glad he was safe.

"I was outside meeting Gloria with the other guys. We came as soon as we heard a gunshot." He gestured to Iris's frozen body. "Did you do this?" he asked.

I nodded. "I kept using magic to freeze the bullets when they came out of the gun, but then it froze Iris, too," I explained.

"I'm glad you were able to take care of everything." He grinned, kissing my forehead. "See, Raven? You are much stronger than you even realized. You just needed the right moment to prove it to yourself."

I melted into him. I hadn't been in his arms in so long.

"Raven, are you okay?" Aiden asked after he let Colton and me have our moment.

"Are all of you okay?" Rhys added, shooting glances at Maddie and Vince.

All of the Darken was here. Everyone who I cared about—who was still alive—was standing around me. The only one who I noticed was still absent was Kane. He *had* to have heard the gunshots if the Darken and Gloria had heard them from outside. There had been so many gunshots, so where was he?

"That was the scariest moment of my life," Maddie said.

"Seriously," Vince agreed. "My life flashed before my eyes."

"We'll be okay," I replied, swallowing hard at the realization that everything was so uncertain. I couldn't allow myself to completely relax. "But we're not in the clear yet, either, so it's still scary. I don't know what to do. I'm pretty sure Iris is going to unthaw any minute. I'm not sure how long she'll be frozen. We have to figure out what we're going to do with her."

"Actually, you did more than just *freeze* Iris," Gloria said as she approached us. "Raven, you *killed* Iris."

"I did?" I swallowed hard, my heart pounding across my chest. That was *the* most relieving thing she could have told me. I didn't feel the slightest bit guilty about killing her. Even though I had never *wanted* to kill anyone in my life, at least I could say with my whole heart that Iris deserved it.

"Really? She's dead in there?" Vince asked, squinting at the Iris-cube.

Needing to prove it to myself, I walked over to the ice cube, noticing that Iris's light eyes were closed. Her body looked even fairer than it usually did.

It looked ghostly white.

"You are the only one who can kill the Triangle," Aiden murmured.

"And elemental magic is one of the only ways for you to kill the Triangle," Gloria explained. "They can die from fire and ice, especially."

I just stared back at Iris.

I had killed her.

I had *actually* killed her.

I hated that it had ended like this, but I was relieved that she was no longer going to be a problem.

But if it was this easy to kill her, it gave me hope that maybe, just maybe, we could kill Milos a little more easily than I had believed we would. For the first time in a long time, I actually had hope that I would be able to avenge Theo's murder.

I couldn't help but feel confused, though. Why had the Triangle always acted like they were so... invincible? Eyeing Iris's frozen body, I realized that it might have all been a lie.

It was either that, or Colton was right. I *was* a lot stronger than I thought I was.

I turned to my mates and Gloria. "Have any of you seen Milos?"

He was next on my list to freeze. Or burn. I wasn't sure which way I wanted to end him. Then again, I didn't know how good I would be at burning things and I knew, for sure, that I could freeze him to death.

"No, we haven't been able to locate him yet," Rhys replied, shaking his head.

Fuck. It looked like locating him was going to be the harder part.

"For some reason, I kind of thought that he would come to Iris's rescue," Vince said.

"It's kind of weird that he didn't," Maddie pointed out.

I hadn't thought of that. They were right.

"I really hope that he didn't see me kill her. I don't want him to know what's coming next for him. I'm hoping that I can catch him off guard. For all we know, he's invisible right now, lurking around us." Goosebumps erupted all over my arms as I glanced down the hallway.

At that moment, the cathedral door burst open, and I jumped. But it wasn't Milos. Kane came rushing into the hallway where we were all standing.

At first, I thought he was coming to me. I thought he was going to hug me and tell me he was glad that I was okay, but he didn't.

He moved past me and rushed over to the ice cube where Iris was.

"You killed her?" He glanced over his shoulder at the rest of us. I could have sworn that he sounded disappointed by that.

I thought I was mistaken at first, but then I saw the look on his face. He was *definitely* disappointed by it.

I wasn't certain, but I also thought he might have even been a little angry.

"Yeah, I killed her," I replied with a nod.

"*How* could you kill her?" Kane pressed.

"I used my magic," I explained.

"No," Kane rolled his eyes and shook his head. "I mean *why* would you kill her?"

"Why wouldn't you want me to? She was going to kill me. She was going to kill my friends if I didn't do anything to stop her." I suddenly felt sick to my stomach over the fact that my husband, my mate, didn't want me to kill the girl who he had known for a long time now had been out to get me. Kane had known that she was Milos's accomplice. Why wouldn't he have wanted her dead? We should have been celebrating together. Instead, it seemed like he was mad at me.

"She was one part of the triangle, Raven. I *needed* her." Kane's eyes flashed with an undeniable anger. "How could you do this to me? Without Iris, I'm going to be less powerful. And I have so many plans."

So, Colton was right. Kane really did want to make this war even worse than it already was. Kane had pretty much just confirmed it.

"I'm afraid this isn't true," Gloria commented. "That isn't how the Triangle works. Even without Iris, both you and Milos Santorini will remain just as powerful as you've always been until the day you both die."

And, judging from the look in Gloria's eyes, I was pretty sure that scared the hell out of her.

CHAPTER 12

"*H*ello, Fallyn." A smile hit Milos's lips as he smiled down at me.

I sat up in bed. "I go by Raven now. It's *Queen* Raven to you."

"I know. I was watching the coronation ceremony. Congratulations on that. Though, I must say that I'm rather surprised by your choice of King," Milos said.

"Why?"

"It's just that you thought *I* would be bad, and then you chose Kane. Of all the werewolves of the land, you thought that traitorous imbecile would make the best King? You didn't have to marry me, but you would have been better off marrying any other werewolf instead of him."

"Kane is strong and powerful. He's part of the Triangle," I argued, even though deep in my heart, I knew that what Milos was saying was right. Kane was a traitor, or he wouldn't have had these secret plans to make this paranormal world war even worse than it already was. He had completely misled me, all so that he could become King and put his plans into action.

"Kane Romero cannot be trusted," Milos said. "I'm worried for you, Raven."

"Worried about me? Since when? *You're* my biggest enemy," I insisted. "Who even let you in here, anyway?"

"Your mother," Milos replied.

"My mother is dead." I paused for a moment. "*Both* of my mothers are dead."

"Actually, you're wrong about that." Milos's black eyes stared back at mine with a look of seriousness behind them. "One of your mothers is alive, and she let me in here so I could reclaim what's mine."

"I'm not yours, and I never will be yours." I swallowed hard.

He took a step closer to me then. "You are mine. You have always been mine, and you always will be mine."

I just narrowed my eyes at him. "Over my dead body."

"Why haven't you done it yet?" Milos asked me.

"Why haven't I done what?"

His black eyes met mine again. "Killed me."

"Are you saying you *want* me to kill you?" I asked him.

"I just don't believe you will," he replied with a shrug. "If you wanted me dead, I would be dead."

"I will," I assured him. "I will get my revenge for you killing Theo."

He stared back at me, confusion written all over his face. "What are you talking about?"

"You heard me. I will kill you, the same way you killed him. You took him away from me. You don't deserve to live."

JAYME MORSE & JODY MORSE

"Raven, you're wrong. I *didn't* kill Theo."

"Yeah, right. You're just saying that. Obviously you *did* kill him."

"I'm being serious with you. If I had killed your mate, I would have taken credit for doing so. I didn't lay a finger on him." He paused. "Nor did I shoot a silver bullet through his heart."

"But if you didn't kill him, then who did?" I asked him.

Before Milos could answer me, he began to fade away from my view.

I JOLTED upright in bed then, my heart pounding against my chest. The sunlight streamed in through the curtains, blinding me as I glanced around the room.

Milos was gone.

I realized that it was just a dream—the type of dream that I knew was going to haunt me for days to come. It had felt so real. It had felt like Milos was actually there with me.

"Raven, are you okay?" Colton whispered from the other side of the bed where he lay next to me. After what had happened after the coronation ceremony with Kane and him being so upset about the fact that I had killed Iris, I knew that I couldn't go back to the King's Quarters with him. It would have just made us get into a fight.

And, truthfully, I was just as disgusted with him as he was with me. I couldn't believe that he was more concerned about carrying out his *plans* and his *power* than he was about me and our child's safety.

Was he forgetting that Iris wouldn't have just killed

me? She would have killed our future child, too. It was almost as though he didn't even care that he was about to become a father.

A part of me wondered if he even *wanted* to.

It didn't matter. Whatever the case was, I was just too angry to go back to his room. But I hadn't wanted to be alone, either, so Colton had come back to my room with me to sleep for the rest of the night. I needed him here. I needed someone who wasn't Kane. Someone who I knew was on my side.

The truth was that I didn't just want Colton. I wanted *all* of my mates—all of them except for Kane.

Colton wrapped his arms around me, and murmured, "You're trembling."

"It was just a dream—a really, *really* bad dream. A nightmare," I explained.

"Do you want to talk about it?" Colton asked.

"Milos was in here with me. He told me that my mother was still alive. He never actually said which mother, but I think he was talking about my biological mother... Queen Lydia." I paused. "Then, he told me that he didn't actually kill Theo."

"Well, I guess the Milos in your dreams is a liar. Probably not much different from the real life Milos," he replied.

"Maybe." I considered it for a long moment before saying, "What if it *wasn't* a dream, Colton?"

He furrowed his brow. "What do you mean? You think he was actually here?" he asked.

"Milos has always been able to enter my mind while I

was awake," I explained. "What if he's figured out a way to come visit me in my dreams now, too?"

"I guess that makes sense," Colton replied with a nod. Then he frowned. "But how could your mother still be alive? Wouldn't she have come to find you by now?"

I shook my head. "Who knows. Queen Lydia probably never would have wanted to see me again after I ran away from her."

He considered it for a moment before shaking his head. "I just don't think it's possible that she's alive. Would she have given up the throne if she was alive?"

"True. I'm not sure why she would have," I replied with a sigh. "You're probably right."

"And we know damn well that Milos is the one who murdered Theo. Who else could have wanted Theo dead?" Colton asked. "Unless Milos was lying to you."

"He seemed so honest. So... genuine. He actually told me that I 'didn't have to marry' him, and that I would have been better off marrying anyone but Kane."

Colton shook his head. "That doesn't sound like something the real Milos would ever say. He wouldn't say that you didn't have to marry him. For some reason, that guy has made it his lifelong mission to drag you down the aisle."

I let out the breath I was holding in. "Are we sure that he hasn't had a change of heart? Maybe he finally understands that I would have never married him, no matter what. Maybe marrying Kane scared him off or something."

"Milos Santorini is never honest or genuine, Raven. *If*

he was in your dream, and that's an extremely big if, he was putting on an act." Colton paused.

"He also told me that Kane is a traitor. He says I chose the wrong werewolf to be King," I added quietly. The last thing I wanted to do was rub salt in the wound or have Colton say *I-told-you-so*, but I thought that might have been enough to convince him that Milos could have really been inside my mind.

"Well, that's not wrong, but still. If I had to guess, I would say that you just had a dream. A really bad dream that feels real," Colton said, pulling me closer to him.

"You're probably right," I replied with a sigh.

"We should probably get up," Colton said. "It's already ten a.m. I'm sure the others are probably already heading downstairs for breakfast."

"I don't want to go downstairs," I replied quietly. The idea of having to face Kane right now sounded absolutely horrible. I needed time to gather my own thoughts after the night before, and I couldn't do that if I had to see him before I was ready. "I really just want to stay in bed all day. Will you lay here with me?"

"Of course I will. Anything you want, my Queen." He leaned in closer to me and kissed me on the neck.

My stomach let out a loud growl then. I may not have wanted to see Kane, but there was no denying that I *was* hungry.

"You sound hungry, and I know you. If you don't eat something soon, you're going to get hangry."

"Me? Never," I replied with a giggle.

"How does breakfast in bed sound?" Colton asked me.

I realized then that he understood the real reason I didn't want to go downstairs yet.

He knew me so well. I knew that if either Aiden or Rhys was here, they would have been able to figure it out, too. Kane was the only one who didn't know me that well. And yet, *he* was the one who I had chosen to marry.

"That sounds great," I told Colton. "Thank you."

He kissed my bare shoulder before climbing out of bed. Pulling his clothes on, he headed out of the room.

Once I was alone in the room with nothing but my thoughts, I stared up at the sheer white fabric of the canopy.

I knew that Colton thought that it had only been a dream, but every part of me was convinced otherwise.

Milos really *had* gotten inside my mind, and he'd left me with more questions than he had answers.

Was my mother really alive?

And if Milos wasn't the one who had killed Theo, then who had?

CHAPTER 13

I thought that becoming Queen would change *everything*, but the truth was that it hadn't.

Whether I was wearing a crown or not, I was still a cyber student at Werewolf Academy, studying to become the most powerful werewolf I could be.

Considering I had already killed Iris, a member of the Triangle, I knew that my power wasn't really in question. I was pretty freaking powerful. I just wasn't sure how easy it would be for me to call on those powers when I *wasn't* in a life-or-death situation. It was something that I would need to work on in the future—so that I was ready whenever an event like that *did* pop up.

I just hoped that I wouldn't have to go through many more situations like that one again.

But, whatever the case, I trusted that Werewolf Academy was preparing me properly. I wanted to make sure that, by the time graduation came, I was ready for any situation my life was going to throw at me.

And now that I was Queen to a King who was eager to sabotage everything I wanted, a king who wanted to do the exact *opposite* of what I wanted, it looked like I really needed to learn more about the history of all of the paranormal races in the world. How else was I going to stop the paranormal world war if I knew nothing about the other paranormal races?

It was somewhat of a relief—and perfect timing—that I had been placed into General Paranormal History, which was my last online class of the day. Now that I knew that Kane was planning something, it was the most important class to me right now. It was the class that I knew I needed to focus my full attention into. I was even trying to do some extra reading on my own.

"Well, class, that about sums up our lesson for today," Professor Wickburn was saying into the monitor. I always dreaded the end of class. I always felt so anxious to learn more. I was on a limited time schedule. "Raven, could you please hang around once all of the other students have left so we can talk in private?"

"Sure," I replied, wondering what she wanted to talk to me about. I knew that it had nothing to do with my grades. I had aced every single test and quiz.

Maybe she just wanted to chat and catch up. The relationship that I had with Caroline Wickburn was so different these days from what it once was. When I first started at Werewolf Academy, we had gotten off on the wrong foot. Her first love was Theo, and even though he had never returned those feelings, she had been jealous of me. But since we had gotten to know another, even more so since Theo had died, she was my ally and one of my biggest supporters. She had been there for me on some of my lowest nights since losing Theo.

I waited until all of the other students had left the virtual classroom and then asked, "So, what's up?"

"I hear that congratulations are in order," she said as she held up a champagne glass.

"You heard about the coronation already?" I asked while I watched her take a sip.

The truth was that I was surprised. Caroline Wickburn lived in Wolflandia, which was pretty far from Nocturne Island. I wasn't sure how she had heard about it so fast.

"Yes, it's been all over the news," she explained.

"Wow. Word really travels fast," I murmured. I supposed that I should have figured that we wouldn't be able to keep it a secret for very long. With the way Luke had gushed about my birth mother, he had probably told whoever would listen that he had performed Queen Lydia's daughter's coronation ceremony—especially considering that our kingdom had been dead before I had shown up to reclaim it.

"I guess so. I wasn't sure if you wanted me to announce to the rest of the classroom that you've become Queen or not." She waved her hand. "I suppose that some of them may have already found out about it, if any of them check the news."

"You can announce it. I don't mind." I shrugged.

"It's kind of fascinating, as a history Professor to watch history in the making. You will be taught about for many years to come," Professor Wickburn said with a smile before her face turned serious. "But I thought the coronation wasn't going to be held until next weekend. Why the change in plans?"

"Kane insisted that we move the coronation up as soon as possible. So, we did," I explained. I paused for a moment, unsure of how much I wanted to disclose with her. Even though I didn't want to tell her that I thought I had fucked up, I couldn't help but feel like I needed to tell *someone*—someone besides Vince and Maddie, who I knew were already biased against Kane. *Everyone* was biased against Kane. I was hoping that Caroline would manage to stay neutral, somehow. "We're already having some... issues."

"I know," Caroline replied sadly, a knowing look in her light blue eyes.

"How do you know?" I asked her through narrowed eyes. *Had she really caught wind of* that, *too?* I was officially kind of... *annoyed,* to say the least. Not at Professor Wickburn, but at whoever had been telling her about things that I thought had been private, or at least within the walls of my castle. Knowing that there might have been a snitch around here made me feel a little uneasy. What other gossip was being let out?

And if she had heard about it, everyone else must have heard about it, too. I hadn't expected that I would lose this much of my privacy when I became Queen. That was one thing that no one had prepared me for.

I just wished I knew how everyone was finding out about things. I didn't believe that it could have been one of my friends or mates… although there was definitely a question mark surrounding Kane.

I just wasn't sure if Kane would have even been worried about getting news out about it when he had more important things to do, like plan his destruction on all of the other paranormal races.

"I had a vision, Raven. I don't have them very often, but when I do, they're always accurate. The things I saw in my vision are the whole reason I wanted to talk with you today," she explained.

I leaned in close to my computer screen, eager to hear about her vision. "What did you see?"

While I was grateful to know what might be coming next for me sometimes, I was really starting to get tired of visions. I knew that Caroline was no Gloria, in the sense that I doubted her visions were ever as accurate as hers, but I couldn't help but be worried about what she was going to tell me next.

"In my vision, you had just given birth to a child."

Crap. So far, so true. I had been keeping my pregnancy a secret from Caroline, too, so it wasn't like she had any way of knowing that part. Unless someone had somehow told her that, too. But I doubted it. Not many people even knew about it yet.

"I'm pregnant," I informed her. "Please keep that between us. I don't want the tabloids to know yet." I knew I could trust her not to say anything to anyone. She hadn't betrayed my trust yet.

She shot me a smile. "Congratulations. Of course I will keep it between us. Now that I know you're pregnant, however, I have even more reason to be convinced that the rest of my vision is true."

"Tell me about the rest of your vision," I pressed. "What happens after I give birth?"

"You were getting married again."

My eyebrows lifted questioningly. "Kane and I decided to renew our vows?"

That seemed like it would be a really odd decision, considering that he hadn't even wanted to use our vows that we had spent so much time on. Or at least, Maddie had spent a lot of time writing mine with me, ensuring that it was perfect. I wasn't sure how much time he had spent on his, for me. Had he even written his own? Whatever the case was, he had seemed very relieved to skip to the "important part" of our wedding.

Maybe that was the whole reason why we were going to have another wedding—because I didn't get the wedding that I deserved, the one that I had always wanted.

A tiny part of me felt like Kane had stolen it from me.

"No. You weren't marrying Kane," Caroline Wickburn replied quietly.

My eyebrows shot up. "S-someone else? Who was it then, if it wasn't Kane?"

"I'm not sure who it was. I just know that it was someone else. His back was turned during the entire vision, so I couldn't figure out who, exactly, it was. All I could see was black hair." She closed her eyes for a few long moments, and I could tell she was replaying the vision in her mind, searching for any details she may have missed the first time around.

"Hmm." None of my other mates had black hair. Aiden's was dark brown, though, so I wondered if it could have been mistaken for black if it was dark out. "Was it daytime or nighttime?"

"Daytime," she replied.

"Was the lighting dim?" I questioned, just to be sure we covered all the bases.

She shook her head. "No, it wasn't dark at all."

So, we could rule Aiden out.

"It wasn't one of my mates, then," I commented.

That meant that Caroline's vision wasn't accurate, because who else would I marry, if not one of my mates? It made no sense.

"You called him your mate," Caroline replied.

How could it have been one of my mates?

Theo had black hair, but there was no way that it could have been him, considering he was, well, dead.

So, either I was about to become mated to someone new, or I was right, and her visions weren't quite as accurate as she seemed to think they were.

I was really hoping it was just that her visions weren't accurate. I didn't want a new mate. I already had enough drama going on with my mates as it was. Well, *one* mate, in particular. Throwing a brand new one into the mix was only going to cause more harm than good.

I couldn't help but worry about my future if this is really what it was going to look like.

"I'm confused. It's not like werewolves can just get divorced like humans can." But one can die, I reminded myself as a wave of nausea washed over me. Kane could die. "How was I marrying someone who wasn't Kane?" I asked.

And what did *any of this* have to do with her knowing that we were having problems?

"Well, here's the thing, Raven. In my vision, Kane was dead."

I swallowed hard. "How did he die?"

But even as the words left my mouth, I already knew the answer.

There was only one way that Kane could be killed since he was one part of the Triangle.

"You killed him," she confirmed.

I WALKED through the rest of the day unsure of how to feel.

I was going to kill my husband. The King. My baby's father.

And then I was going to remarry. I was going to choose a new King. A new black-haired King who was going to be my mate.

Aside from the fact that I was going to be welcoming a new mate into my life, there was something else that bothered me about Caroline's vision.

Why would I *choose* this new black-haired mate to become King instead of one of my other current mates? Why hadn't I learned my lesson?

Going through everything that I'd been going through with Kane had made me fully understand that I had chosen the wrong mate to be King. If I had to do it all over again, I had thought that I would have chosen one of my current mates. Aiden, Colton, and Rhys would have made good Kings—much better Kings than Kane ever could.

So why was I going to do the opposite?

Future me seemed really dumb.

I sure hoped she had her reasons.

I kept wondering who the hell it could have been. Was it possible that maybe just one part of Caroline Wickburn's vision had been off?

Only one werewolf came to mind who had black hair, and that was Milos. There was no way in hell I was going to marry Milos, so we could rule him out.

Or could we?

What if he somehow forced me down the aisle. Or what if it was somehow the best thing for the paranormal world war if I married Milos?

I just couldn't imagine ever being mated to him.

I wasn't going to lie, though. Ever since my dream about Milos, I didn't have the same desire or urgency to kill him as I once had.

Knowing that there was a possibility that he might not have been the one who had murdered Theo made me feel less hatred towards him.

I needed to direct all of my hatred at Theo's actual killer.

I just wasn't sure who else would have wanted my mate dead.

A thought crossed my mind then, something that I hadn't even wanted to consider before now.

Could it have been Kane?

JAYME MORSE & JODY MORSE

It would have made so much sense if it had been him.

I tried to remember where he had been at the end of the year festival when the shots rang out, but everything about that day was a big blur in my mind.

I tried to replay that day in my head. I needed to go over the way it happened, to see if I had missed anything.

As the Tilt-a-Whirl came to a halt, I climbed off. Not even bothering to wait for my friends, I began to make way back into the crowd of people, who were swarming all around me.

I scanned the area for my mates. Colton and Rhys had just been at the food stands moments before, while Theo and Aiden had been playing darts at one of the game stands. I wasn't even sure where I had seen Kane last.

But now, none of them were anywhere to be seen.

A weird feeling came over me then. I could feel it deep in my gut. It was the wolfy intuition again.

Something wasn't right.

My heart pounded against my chest as a million emotions— panic, fear, worry—swarmed through my veins.

But this time, it was different. This time, I knew these emotions weren't mine alone. No, these emotions belonged to my mates. It was their energy I was feeling. I could feel their panic, fear, and worry as it shot through me like the fireworks that were being set off in the distance.

Speaking of the fireworks, they were supposed to meet me here when they started. But none of them were anywhere in sight.

I wasn't even sure what was happening. All I knew was that something was going on... something that I could feel wasn't supposed to be going on.

That was when I heard the sound of the gunshot ring out in the distance, and I felt it: the pain. It wasn't slow or gradual. No, it completely tore through me; it felt like something had been ripped away from me. It was as if a piece of my soul was being torn out of me, and I knew exactly what that meant.

One of my mates had died.

As I fell to my knees sobbing and wailing, Maddie and Vince came to my side, asking if I was okay. I tried to answer them, but I couldn't even form words, let alone sentences.

All I could see was red.

I didn't even have to wonder who had killed my mate, because I already knew the answer. I could feel it in my bones.

I made a promise to myself then. I was going to do the one thing I had wanted to do from the first day I had set foot on the Werewolf Academy campus.

I was going to kill Milos Santorini, once and for all.

"Raven? Are you okay?" Vince asked, kneeling on the ground next to me.

I couldn't move. I couldn't swallow the lump that had formed in my throat. I couldn't even breathe.

"Honey, what's wrong? What happened?" His voice was dripping with confusion.

Choking on my tears, I shook my head. "No. One of my mates..." I swallowed hard, trying to get the words out. "One of my mates is dead."

Vince wrapped his arms around me in a loose embrace. "I'm sorry. How do you know?"

"Because," I replied quietly. "It feels like a part of me just died, too."

* * *

MY FEET COULD BARELY CARRY me as we scanned the Werewolf Academy campus for my mates. We were able to locate Aiden and Colton.

That meant that it could have been Rhys, Theo, or Kane.

My heart hurt thinking about which of them I had lost. Physically and emotionally, I knew that it wouldn't make much of a difference which one had been killed. My heart ached for all five of them.

But deep down, I had already made a decision on who I wanted to spend the rest of my life with.

I had decided that it was him: the one who I had initially been attracted to, the first one who I had fallen for.

If I hadn't kissed the others, maybe it would have only ever been me and him. I couldn't help but feel like destiny had thought the two of us belonged together, and so it was time. Time to choose him, once and for all.

But I had a really, really bad feeling deep in my gut.

"Let's go back to the house," Colton suggested. "I thought I saw Rhys head in that direction."

I swallowed hard. That was where the gunshots had sounded like they were being fired from.

The truth was that I was afraid to go back to the house. Downright terrified, really.

Because not only was I about to find out which one of my mates had been killed, but I was also pretty sure I was about to come face-to-face with Milos Santorini. Mentally, I wasn't ready for that—not when he had just taken someone who I considered to be everything from me.

But still, my feet allowed me to follow Colton and the others *back to the house, my heart pounding against my chest like a snare drum with every step we took.*

When we got there, we found the front door had been left open.

My stomach lurched as we climbed the front steps.

When we stepped inside the house, I saw his body laying there on the floor. The blood was splattered all around him, and it didn't take a rocket scientist to see that his chest wasn't moving up and down.

And I didn't hear his heartbeat. Not as I moved closer to his body, and not even as I pressed my ear to his chest as the tears poured from my eyes.

He was dead.

Theo was dead.

Colton came to my side and held me then as I shook, crying and screaming.

Before I even knew what was happening, Aiden came to the other side of me, wrapping his arms around me and pulling me away from Theo's body.

"Search the area for Milos," Aiden said.

"Okay," Colton agreed with a nod. He began to do a full search of the house as I just continued to cry.

As I heard the sound of the back door opening and closing, Aiden kissed me on the forehead. "I'm not letting you go. I need you right now, just as much as I know you need me."

I nodded into his shoulder.

When Colton returned, he shook his head, "There's no sign of Milos anywhere."

"We have to find him," I said through my tears. "We have to get revenge."

"We'll worry about that later. Right now, we need to worry about removing Theo's body."

I began to sob as he said the words.

Aiden glanced over at Colton. "Did you really have to word it like that?"

"Sorry. I wasn't sure how else to put it," he replied quietly.

"We'll help you clean up the mess," Vince offered. "But we should probably get Raven out of here."

"That sounds like a good idea," Maddie agreed.

"I want to go to sleep," I said quietly. Even though I wanted to get revenge, right now I just wanted to pretend like this was all a really bad dream.

"Then to sleep we'll go." Aiden carried me to my bedroom and climbed into the bed with me, where we both began to cry together.

Colton came into the room and sat down at the edge of the bed.

Rhys eventually followed, perching on my vanity chair.

We all cried together.

I REALIZED THEN that Kane was the only one who had been missing that night as we all grieved Theo's death together as a pack. Kane should have been there for me. For all of us.

Later on, he claimed that he had been at the festival looking for all of us. He had obviously heard the gunshot, but he didn't think it had anything to do with any of us.

Now, I couldn't help but wonder if the reason he had been M.I.A. through all of this was because he was actually guilty.

I wondered if the whole reason he wasn't there for us that night was because he didn't want to be. Because he was *happy* that Theo was gone.

So, that left me with one big question that I didn't know the answer to.

If what Milos Santorini had said in my dream was true, was it possible that it was actually Kane who killed Theo?

CHAPTER 14

The next couple of days passed by slowly. I spent my days trying to avoid Kane at all costs. The last thing I wanted was to be around him anytime soon. I kept sleeping with one of my other mates each night and always had them bring meals to me so that I wouldn't have to see him or interact with him.

I couldn't help but feel betrayed by him, to say the least.

First, there was the wedding. He had completely ruined it just because he didn't want to risk the chance of me deciding not to go through with it if we pushed it back to even a day later. He didn't want to give me the chance to back out and choose another mate to become king instead of him. Then there was the fact that he had intentionally moved up the coronation ceremony—a ceremony that I felt was supposed to have been more for *me* than for him—and ruined that, too, all for his own selfish gain. I was the rightful heir to the throne. Kane wouldn't have even become King if I didn't choose him. The fact that he'd had the audacity to think that he could push up the ceremony to a time that *he* had chosen was a move that I knew I would always hold against him. It wasn't something that I would have ever been able to forgive.

That brought me to *another* unforgivable thing I could add to the ever-growing list of *Things I Can Never Forgive Kane For*: the fact that he had actually been upset about me killing Iris.

But the biggest problem of all was that he had made me not trust him. I knew that he had shattered my trust in him so badly that going forward, I could never trust him. Right now, it didn't seem fixable—and maybe I didn't *want* it to be fixable, because what if he *had* killed Theo?

But what if he *hadn't*? What if he was innocent of that part?

No matter how much I thought about it, I just couldn't seem to figure out what his motive could have been. I knew that the two of them had always rivaled over who was the Alpha of the pack, but would that have been reason enough for Kane to kill him?

Even though fate had technically chosen *me* to be the Alpha of the pack, there had been an unspoken agreement between all of the Darken that Kane was the Alpha since he had returned unexpectedly. I hadn't fought Kane over the spot because I didn't feel like I was the best-suited for Alpha, anyway. I didn't *want* to be the Alpha, even though that was what the universe apparently wanted for me. My personality was a little bit too lenient; I was horrible at bossing people around—especially the ones I loved. Kane

was the exact opposite of me, and his dominant personality had always made me believe that he was a better
Alpha than I ever could have been. Everything about him
just demanded authority. Kane was a force to be reckoned
with (which was yet another reason why I had thought he
would make the best King).

Was it possible that Kane might have killed Theo
because he had thought he was in competition for
becoming Alpha? Even though anything was possible, it
just didn't seem to add up when he was already acting as
our Alpha.

Another possibility entered my mind then.

Was it possible that Kane had somehow figured out
that I was going to choose Theo? If he had known that I
would choose him, that would have meant that he'd
known that Theo would become the next King of the
wolves.

Had Kane wanted to make sure that Theo wouldn't get
in the way of him becoming King?

ON FRIDAY AFTERNOON, there was a knock at my bedroom
door. It could have been *any* of my mates, considering
that I had been avoiding all of them.

Even though I had originally wanted Colton, Aiden,
and Rhys's company, I kind of just wanted to be left alone
now.

I needed to be alone to process my thoughts.

That meant that I had started ignoring *all* of my mates.

"Who is it?" I called out, crossing my fingers and toes

that it wasn't Kane. So far, he had been giving me a lot of space. I was almost offended at how much space he had been giving me. I was sure that it was clear that I hadn't wanted to be around him, but I hadn't actually asked him to give me space. Part of me sort of expected him to try a little harder to chase me. It kind of felt like a slap in the face that he hadn't even bothered to try to talk to me or come see me.

It was almost as if he was completely okay with not speaking to me. And I didn't like that. He was supposed to be my mate. We had gotten married. Was he forgetting that we were newlyweds? And even though I had only married him so that I could become Queen, the truth was that I loved him… and I wanted to believe that the feeling was a mutual one. But I was pretty sure he had used *me* more than I had used him.

So, even though I had *wanted* him to chase me, I also still didn't want to have to answer the door if it was him.

To my relief, Maddie was the one who spoke up from the other side of the door. "It's me," she said.

Muting my TV, I let out the sigh that I hadn't even known I had been holding in. "Come in."

She opened the door and stepped into the room, shutting it quietly behind her. "Hey."

I saw her eyes searching for me under the pile of blankets I was laying under.

I waved at her, even though my fingers were covered with orange powder from the Doritos I had been snacking on. My stash of snacks was dwindling down. I had already run out of the packages of powdered sugar donuts, chocolate chip cookies, and barbeque-flavored chips. It wouldn't be long before I would have to ask someone to bring me more food. I should have been conserving what I had left, but I couldn't help it. I was so hungry.

I couldn't tell if I was eating my feelings, eating for two, or what.

For the past two days, I had been wearing the light pink robe with silver embroidery on it that read *Queen.* It had been a bridal shower gift from Vince.

Honestly? I looked like a hot mess... but *only* if we were talking about "hot" in terms of temperature. I totally looked like I had been living in a humid jungle or something, with as frizzy as my hair looked. Apparently, that was what happened when I didn't brush it for a few days and spent most of my time laying on it.

But, whatever. I was glad it was just Maddie instead of someone that I would have felt uncomfortable with seeing me like this.

"Raven, you look..." Maddie trailed off, as if she was trying to put her thoughts into words.

Or maybe she was just trying to be nice.

My appearance had left her speechless. That was apparently how bad I looked. I wasn't sure if she had ever even seen me like this.

"Like a total bum?" I offered.

"Something like that." She sat down carefully on the edge of the bed, maintaining a safe distance from the Doritos crumbs that littered the white and gold comforter. "Are you okay?"

The truth was that I wasn't exactly sure how to answer

her. In a way, I supposed that even I didn't know the answer to that.

So, instead, I played dumb. "Why wouldn't I be?" I asked.

"Well, I know you've gone through a lot of traumatic events recently," she replied. "Killing Iris—"

"*Defending myself from* Iris," I corrected her. "It's all about perspective. I don't care that I killed her."

Most of the time, that was true. Until a flash of a memory from happier times popped into my head and I couldn't stop thinking about it. She was my first real friend at Werewolf Academy. The two of us had been so close early on, before everything went to shit. Before she became a horrible friend.

Before she had betrayed me.

But it was hard not to miss all of the time we had spent together. All of our sleepovers, Netflix nights, and track meets were fond memories of mine. We even managed to have fun while we studied for our classes or did homework.

It was just such a shame that it had ended this way.

"Right, of course. I'm not saying that you were wrong for killing her. It needed to happen. You protected *all* of us. I just meant that it has to weigh heavy on your shoulders. And between that and realizing that Kane isn't really on your side—"

"Wait," I interrupted. "You think he's not on my side, too?"

Maddie's eyes met mine. "I mean…" she trailed off with a shrug. "Pretty much."

"Great," I said with a sigh. "Does everyone else think that, too?"

Maddie tucked her lips together. She looked like she didn't want to say anything at first, but then she blurted, "It's just that he was so upset that you killed Iris. If he was on your side, wouldn't he have wanted what was best for you and the baby? Why doesn't he?!" There was a look of anger on her face.

"Lovely," I said with an eye roll. "It's bad enough that *I* think he's not on my side. Now I have all of you watching me and judging me for staying with someone who isn't on my side."

Hearing her point of view also made me feel sort of sad. It was like she was confirming it for me. I couldn't just chalk it up to my imagining it anymore. Kane really *wasn't* on my side, if all of them could see through him.

"We're not judging you at all. You're in a really tough situation," Maddie said, her voice soft.

I nodded as a lump formed in my throat. I could feel the tears starting to build up in my eyes. I didn't want them to start falling now.

Even though I felt like he had betrayed me on so many levels, there was a large part of me that still loved him.

I knew it was because we shared a mate bond and now a marriage bond. The two of us weren't meant to be apart; we could *never* be apart. Not even if it was what was best for me.

Knowing that he wasn't on my side, even though we shared that deep of a connection with one another… Well, it just sucked. How could he be so heartless?

"I also know that you're probably afraid, since no one

has found Milos yet," Maddie continued, her voice interrupting my thoughts.

"I'm not afraid," I said, and for the first time, it was the truth when it came to Milos. Now that I believed with my entire heart that Milos hadn't actually murdered Theo, I couldn't help but fear him slightly less. Of course I didn't like him, and after him kidnapping me, I didn't trust him —not even a little bit. But I had spent so much time thinking that he had killed my parents *and* Theo, only to learn that he hadn't killed any of them. He had become less of a monster in my mind ever since I found that out.

Maddie stared at me with wide eyes. "We all understand if you're afraid. Milos is scary. Vince and I are afraid, too."

"Don't be. I don't think he would actually do anything to hurt either of you," I insisted. I actually believed that. He had no reason to try to hurt them.

"If you're not afraid of him, then why have you been hanging out in your room so much? You're becoming a hermit."

"It's not that I'm afraid of Milos. It's just that I don't want to face Kane. Not yet, anyway. I'm just not ready. So, instead, I've been passing my time watching paranormal reality TV. You have to watch *The Fae Wedding Planner*, by the way. It's so much better than *Say Yes to the Dress*."

"Okay. I'll watch it sometime," Maddie replied with a nod. "But you can't stay in bed forever, Raven. You're the *Queen*. You have shit to do—things that you won't accomplish by lying in bed all day like you've been doing." She paused. "You know, like making this war actually stop."

"And like murdering Kane," I added with a sigh.

That was part of why I was hiding out in my room, too. I wasn't ready to face the truth.

"*What?*" My best friend glanced over at me with wide eyes. "I thought you didn't like the idea of murdering him."

"So, between you and me, Caroline Wickburn had this vision about me," I explained. "She saw that I would end up murdering Kane and that I would get married to another mate—a guy with black hair. I don't know who that could be. I guess I'm going to end up becoming mated to someone new."

Maddie cupped a hand over her mouth.

I glanced over at her with wide eyes. "What's wrong?"

"It's just that I had the same dream. Well… *sort of*. I didn't dream that you were going to murder Kane. But I did dream that Kane died and we were at his funeral, and then later on, I was walking down the aisle at your wedding. I couldn't see the groom's face, but he definitely had black hair."

"Okay, that's freaky. Caroline Wickburn didn't see his face, either."

"I really wonder what that means," Maddie commented.

"That I'm marrying a guy without a face?" I shrugged.

"I'm pretty sure he has a face." She rolled her eyes. "I just wonder why neither of us could see it."

"Me, too." I swallowed hard. "Do you think this dream is true?"

"What are the odds that Caroline Wickburn and I both basically saw the same thing?" Maddie asked.

"I know." That was exactly what scared me about it.

The idea that Kane was going to end up dead scared me enough. No matter what had happened between the two of us or what would happen between us going forward, he was still my mate. But knowing that I was probably going to be the reason he ended up dead…

Well, the truth was that scared the shit out of me.

CHAPTER 15

*L*ater that night, all of my mates, aside from Kane, sat at the dining table with me.

Maddie's talk with me had done some good. She convinced me that I would feel a lot better if I showered and put on some makeup and a cute outfit.

She was right. I felt more like myself again. I felt so much more confident in the lacy light peach off the shoulder dress with the sweetheart bodice that she had picked out for me after wearing a robe for so many days.

I was pretty sure that Kane must have gotten the hint that I had been avoiding him, so now he was going out of his way to avoid me now, too.

It was all turning into such a childish game, and, frankly, I was over it. If he wanted to keep playing games, he was going to be the only participant. I was done with it.

But I *had* asked all of my mates besides Kane to join me for dinner, so I was relieved that he hadn't decided to crash the party (that he hadn't even known was going to be taking place).

As one of the servants brought our bowls of heaping, colorful salads out to us, I glanced around the table. I didn't want to have to do this, but… it was time.

I couldn't wait any longer. The longer I waited, the worse it would be.

"You guys? There's something I really need to tell you," I told them.

I was so nervous. How were they going to react?

"What is it, Raven?" Rhys's eyes darted over to meet mine. Colton set his fork down and then glanced over at me. Aiden's gaze settled on mine as all three of them waited for me to break the news.

"There's no easy way for me to say this, but I want you all to know. I want you to hear it from me." I paused for a moment, swallowing hard. Were they going to be angry? I couldn't imagine how I would take the news if it was the other way around. I would have been completely heartbroken. "I'm pregnant."

"I see." Colton glanced away from me. I might have only been imagining it, but I could have sworn that his gray eyes had glossed over with tears. Seeing how upset he was made my heart hurt.

"Congratulations," Rhys said, even though I could tell that his smile was forced. I could see the sadness behind his dark blue eyes that were struggling to hold my gaze.

When I glanced over at Aiden, I couldn't help but notice the red circles that had blossomed on his cheeks. He looked really freaking pissed.

A long, uncomfortable silence hung in the air between

us. My eyes flickered between the three of them, hoping that someone would say something, because I was at a loss for words.

This was one of the hardest conversations I had ever had to have.

Finally, Colton's voice sliced through the silence. "When is the baby due?"

"I don't know. It could be any day now."

"You're that far along?" Rhys looked surprised and even more hurt that I hadn't bothered to tell them until now.

I really sucked.

"Yeah, I've known for a while now," I admitted.

"And you didn't think to tell us?" Colton asked, narrowing his eyes at me. I realized then that he was just as pissed as Aiden was; he was just doing a better job of hiding it.

"I was just trying to process it myself," I explained. "It wasn't how I was expecting my life to turn out. I mean, I'm a senior at Werewolf Academy, and I'm pregnant," I paused before deciding *not* to add that I was pregnant by someone who I really didn't want to have a kid with. Clearing my throat, I went on, "I was also trying to get over Theo's death while dealing with this. It's just been a lot."

"Aww." Rhys shot a sympathetic look in my direction and reached for my hand to give it a small squeeze.

"The bigger question is who's the father?" Aiden spoke up then, his voice gruff. As mad as he was, I could tell that he was having a hard time holding it together.

Ugh. This was the hardest part to share, the part that I had seriously been dreading.

I knew that none of them were going to be happy about the answer, but I couldn't lie to them about it, either.

When I didn't respond, Aiden nodded. "Got it. It's his."

"Aiden—" I started to say, but he shook his head.

"You know, I should have expected this. We all should have been expecting it, Raven. Because at the end of the day, you chose him. You decided to marry him and make him King. Having his child is just another step towards making this situation more permanent than it already was. But do you want to know my honest opinion?" His honey brown eyes met mine.

"Let's hear it." I braced myself for whatever he was about to say next. I had a feeling it was going to be really harsh… and I couldn't even say that I didn't deserve it. He had the right to be upset. He was allowed to express himself.

I just hoped that I would be able to handle him lashing out at me.

"The day you chose him, it was a slap in the face for the rest of us. All three of us love you with everything we have. We would kill for you, Raven," Aiden told me, completely surprising me with the softness of his voice. He wasn't even lashing out at me. But then again, I wasn't sure why I was so surprised by that. Aiden wasn't Kane. Kane was the one who would have lashed out at me. As Aiden's eyes held mine while he waited for my reaction, he asked, "But can you say the same about Kane?"

I opened my mouth to speak, but I wasn't sure what to say. So, instead, I just said nothing at all.

Kane had made it really hard for me to defend him. There wasn't even a point in trying to defend him. It was a lost cause, because I knew that Aiden was right.

I knew that now, but it was too late. The damage had already been done and there was nothing I could do to change any of it.

"In case you're wondering, the answer is no. Kane doesn't love you. And you know how I know that?" Aiden's eyes locked on mine. "Because Kane isn't capable of loving *anyone*."

I didn't think that part was true. I didn't believe that Kane wasn't capable of loving anyone. I believed that Kane *did* love me, in his own way. He had to have.

"I'm his mate," I said quietly. "That has to count for something."

He shook his head. "It doesn't—not when it comes to Kane. He's a narcissistic asshole. He doesn't love anyone but himself. He never has, and he never will. It doesn't matter that you're his mate or that you're carrying his child. He will never love you, Raven." His eyes met mine. "You will never be enough for Kane. And I'm afraid that if we don't do something to stop him, you're going to end up just like Miriam."

"He had good reason to kill Miriam, Aiden. I talked to him about it," I replied quietly. But even as I spoke the words, I knew that didn't make up for the fact that he had betrayed me in other ways. He had still cared more about keeping Iris alive than he had about me and our unborn baby. He had prioritized his power over our family.

"Is there ever a good reason to kill your wife?" Rhys asked with raised eyebrows. He looked completely horrified at the suggestion that Miriam deserved what Kane had done to her.

"There are two sides to every story, Raven. Unfortunately, Miriam isn't alive to tell her side of things, so we'll never actually know the truth. You'll only ever know Kane's version of it." Aiden's honey brown eyes held mine. "For the record, Kane isn't exactly what you would call honest. He *did* fake his own death," he reminded me.

I had never thought about it that way before, but he was right. Honesty wasn't exactly Kane's best quality. I had never really considered that he might have lied about the real reason he had killed Miriam, but maybe Aiden was right. Maybe Kane's version of things wasn't the truth. Why had I been so accepting of what he had told me?

I knew why. It was because I didn't want to believe otherwise. I didn't want to believe that he was a monster.

It was no joke that love was blinding.

I knew, though, that I just hadn't been willing to take the blindfold off. I had clung to the idea of Kane so hard.

"On that note, I'm going to take a walk." Aiden rose to his feet then. Glancing over at me, he added, "Congratulations, by the way. I know you'll be a great mom."

Then, without saying another word, he stormed out of the room. I flinched as he slammed the dining room door shut behind him.

Even though I had been expecting this sort of reaction, I felt like I was going to cry.

Rhys shot a sympathetic glance in my direction. "Don't

let his words bother you, Raven. He's just letting his emotions get the better of him."

"He's not completely wrong, though. It *was* a slap in the face for you to choose Kane," Colton said quietly. "We were here first. We were here *for you* before you even knew he existed. I'm sorry. Maybe I shouldn't be telling you how I feel. What's done is already done. No one can change the past, and you clearly already made your decision. You decided, out of all of us, who would be the better husband, better king, better mate, and better father to your child. I can't help but think that you chose wrong. It doesn't matter what I think. But ultimately, you wrecked us. And you don't even seem to care that you wrecked us."

"I wrecked us?" I questioned him. This was the other part of the conversation that I had been dreading. It was the part where I was going to learn where I stood with them. I really didn't want to question it further, but I needed to know.

Maybe I didn't even need confirmation from them. I glanced down at the tattoo and the shattered paw print. It was all the proof that I needed to know that I really *had* shattered us.

"We all really loved you." Colton rose to his feet then, too. I couldn't help but notice his choice in words: *loved*, as in past tense.

As in he no longer loved me. None of them did anymore.

Tears welled up in my eyes.

He was about halfway to the door when he glanced over his shoulder at me. As if he had read my mind, he said, "We will still love you. We will always love you, but this really sucks, and I hate that you did this to us."

As he left the room, I was left alone with Rhys.

"I don't... get it." I swallowed hard. "How does this baby with Kane change anything any more than it already did? You all already knew he was my husband. He's still my husband. The marriage bond is already there, and it's permanent. It's as permanent as a child is, except a child grows up and will leave to go live its life or start a family eventually. I can never leave Kane. I'm with him forever."

"I don't know. I think we were all sort of hoping that this would only be a temporary thing."

"How would it have only been temporary? Marriage bonds are forever," I pointed out again.

Rhys's eyes moved over to meet mine as he poked the hard-boiled egg in his salad with a fork. I noticed all of the other uneaten salads on the table. It was so out of the norm for my mates to lose their appetites. It hardly ever happened. "This is going to sound horrible, but I think we were all sort of hoping that you would find a reason to kill Kane in the end."

If only they knew I still had reason to believe that this still could happen.

"You never know. I might still end up killing him." I shrugged.

"You won't." He shook his head confidently. "Please don't get our hopes up for no reason. I know that you wouldn't actually go through with something like that."

"How do you figure?" I couldn't help but feel sort of... *offended*. I was the only one in this world who had the ability to kill Kane. Why didn't Rhys think I was capable

135

of doing so? I'd had no problem killing Iris. It should have been just as easy to kill Kane.

"Because it was already going to be hard enough for you to kill him, considering he's your mate *and* you married him," Rhys replied. "But now that you're carrying his baby… Well, I just know you, Raven. You don't have a mean bone in your body. I can't see you killing the father of your child." He shrugged and then speared a tomato with his fork, and popped it into his mouth.

As I picked up my own fork, I thought about it for a moment. What he was saying wasn't wrong—not entirely, anyway.

I didn't want to take the father of my child away from him or her. But one thing that I knew all too well myself was that you couldn't miss what you'd never had—the same way I hadn't missed my biological parents all of these years.

I made a decision then.

If I was going to murder Kane, I had to do it before our baby was born… or I could never do it at all.

CHAPTER 16

*W*hen I went downstairs for breakfast the next morning, Lana, one of the maids, came over to me. "Your Majesty, the Darken pack left a note for you."

A note? That was completely out of character for them.

"Thank you," I replied as I took the piece of paper from her with a shaky hand.

I swallowed hard, completely nervous and afraid to see what the note could have been about. I wondered if all three of them were breaking up with me. I wondered if they were already getting far, far away from me. It wouldn't have even surprised me after the way things had gone the night before. I had hurt all of them so much.

Unfolding the note, I stared down at the words that had been written on it. I immediately recognized Colton's handwriting.

Raven,

. . .

Rhys, Aiden, and I are going hunting for the weekend. We need to hunt, and we also need to let go of some stress and take our mind off of things. Don't worry. We're coming back. We won't be going far. We plan to stick to Nocturne Island. We'll return late tonight or early tomorrow morning.

There isn't great service on that part of the island. If you need to communicate with us when we're gone, take off the necklace.

Love you,

Colton

I reread the way he had written *Love you* a few more times. I touched my necklace gently, smiling at the fact that he had felt the need to remind me about how to get in touch with them.

Even though I knew that hunting was probably the best thing for them, I also couldn't help but feel sort of nervous for two reasons:

1). They were leaving me alone with Kane. Sure, my friends were residing in the castle, but still. If something were to happen, I would want my other mates to be here for me, too; and

2). Milos was still out there on the island somewhere.

The idea of him running into them—the idea of him *killing them*—made me feel sick to my stomach.

3). And it was a really, really bad sign that I was worried about them leaving me alone with my own husband. My own mate.

I knew that I shouldn't let myself worry about the guys while they were on their trip. At the end of the day, the Darken had been around for a very long time. They knew how to take care of themselves. They were strong guys. They had it under control.

Everything would be okay, both inside and outside of the castle.

At least, I hoped it would.

* * *

Later that night, I was working on my Werewolf Literature homework in my bedroom quarters when there was a knock at the door.

"Come in," I called out, fully expecting it to be Maddie and Vince to drag me out of bed to go hang out in the castle movie theater or bowling alley, which were their two favorite spots lately.

But to my surprise, it was Kane who stood on the other side of the door.

He was holding a bouquet of bright yellow daisies.

"May I come in?" His emerald green eyes locked on mine.

I thought about it for a moment. If he thought that

some flowers were going to make up for everything, he was out of his mind. It was a little embarrassing that he thought it would be that easy.

But at the same time, I knew that there was no way that we could go without talking forever. Whether I liked it or not, I had chosen him to be my King. We were married. And I was having his baby. As much as I wanted to tell him to go away, I couldn't bring myself to.

So, I nodded. "Yeah, come in."

Placing the flowers on my nightstand, he sat down on a gold accent chair across from my bed. "Can we talk?"

"What is there to say?" I asked him.

"Well, there is the fact that you've been avoiding me," Kane replied quietly.

"Yeah, well. Maybe next time you should think about who really matters to you in a life-or-death situation: someone who you believe will give you extra power, or your wife and unborn child." I stared at him evenly.

"Raven, I'm sorry. I didn't mean to make you feel like you aren't important to me, because you are. You're my mate. You mean the absolute world to me." He reached out and touched my hand gently, but I recoiled from him.

Flowers and phrases like "you mean the absolute world to me" wouldn't fix this.

"Kane, why did you want to push up the coronation ceremony? Don't tell me it's because of Gloria. I know she didn't have a vision about us needing to become King and Queen faster." I stared at him accusingly.

"Actually, you're right. It was the only way I knew to get you to agree to go through our coronation earlier than expected," Kane admitted. "I couldn't think of another excuse. It was the best that I could come up with."

"Wait, you're *admitting* that you lied to me?" I was sort of surprised, to be honest. I had figured that he would deny it.

"Yeah. I know it's going to sound a little crazy—and maybe it *is* crazy—but I was just so anxious to get the coronation ceremony over with. After the way Iris and Milos practically crashed our wedding, I was afraid that if we had our coronation the way we had been planning, they would crash that, too—or worse. I thought that if we did things early, it would be so unexpected and catch them off guard, and then we wouldn't need to worry about them ruining that, too."

I just stared back at him for a long moment. Everything that he had just said actually made sense.

Was it possible that all of this was *true?*

Maybe Kane hadn't moved the coronation up because he wanted to make the war worse. Maybe this really was the real reason.

It seemed so believable… and not only just believable, but also really smart. Or, it would have been smart if Iris hadn't found out about it, anyway.

"You could have just told me that at the time," I said finally.

"I was afraid that you wouldn't agree with me. I was afraid that you cared about sending the perfect coronation photos to the tabloids and having the videographers there. I thought that having the perfect coronation just meant something to you. I thought that you wanted to have the total Princess experience."

"I've never cared about any of that," I paused as I thought it over. Okay. Maybe I had cared about that a little bit. But Maddie was definitely the one who had cared about all of that more than I ever had.

"I think you did," Kane insisted.

Ignoring him, I said, "All I want is for this war to end, and for everyone who I love to get through it in one piece."

"I get it," he replied with a nod.

"I want life to go back to normal again." I sighed. "I want to go back to Werewolf Academy."

"You do?" His eyebrows shot up questioningly.

I nodded. "Yeah. I miss it there."

"But you have the castle now—the throne. What would you want to go back there for?" He sounded genuinely confused.

I shrugged. "This castle has been vacant for so long. Does it even matter if we stay?"

"Of course it matters. This is our new home," Kane said firmly. "There's no reason for you to finish your courses at Werewolf Academy. You can drop out now, if you want. You have no use for them anymore."

"Why would I want to drop out? The school is supposed to help train me to be the most powerful were-wolf I can be."

He stared back at me as if he was trying to make sense of what I had just said. "Raven, you're Queen of the wolves. There isn't a more powerful female werewolf in this world than you. You're already on top. You're as powerful as you can get."

"I just feel like I have so much learning left to do." I

shrugged. Glancing over at him, I asked the question that was on my mind. "You really didn't want to move the coronation up so that you could make this war worse?"

Kane's lips formed a flat line. "Why would you even think that?"

I shrugged. "It was just something that crossed my mind."

The last thing I was about to do was rat out Gloria for telling Colton this. I had to make Kane believe that I had thought this up entirely on my own.

"I can't believe that you would ever think that of me." His green eyes met mine. "I know that you might not believe this, but I've always wanted to protect you, Raven. Ever since the day I helped you escape from the tower the Queen was holding you prisoner in on what was supposed to have been the day of you and Milos's wedding, I have always wanted to keep you safe."

"Actually, I have a question for you about that day," I told him. "Why were you just hanging out in my mother's tower that day? It seems like too much of an odd coincidence for you to have just been there to rescue me that day. There's no doubt that you were my knight in shining armor, but how did you just happen to ride in on your white horse and save me when I actually *needed* saving? It had worked out almost too perfectly."

"I always wanted to be your husband," Kane replied.

"Was that the first time we met? That day in the prison tower?" I asked him.

He nodded. "Yes, that was formally the first time we had ever met. But I was keeping an eye on you for a while. I often used an invisibility spell to sneak into the castle and…" He trailed off. "If I tell you this, you must promise not to judge me."

"I promise," I assured him with a nod.

"I would just watch you. You were so beautiful. There was nothing I wanted more than to be with you."

"But *why*? Why did you want to marry me *so* bad?"

"You don't remember?"

A memory that I had unlocked about a year ago, one that I hadn't thought about again, until this moment, came rushing back to me then:

We fell to a pile on the ground, and I saw him for the very first time.

He wore his dark brown hair short, and he had a scruffy-looking beard with sideburns. It was the type of beard the Queen would have called improper.

What I noticed the most was the size of him. His arms were so muscular that I thought his fitted jacket might tear right open. Even through the material of his jacket, I could see that he was pure muscle.

My eyes met his then for the first time, and my breath caught in my throat. He had the most beautiful emerald green eyes I had ever seen in my life. And when he looked at me, all I could feel was pure lust. It was as if his eyes were pouring deep into my soul.

No one had ever looked at me that way before, not even Nicholas, the only guy who I had ever loved.

But the way this beautiful stranger stared at me made me feel things I had never felt before.

I shouldn't have felt this way. It had been less than twenty-

four hours since Nicholas had died. There was no way I could have been feeling things for someone else already.

And yet, I was.

Reaching over, he brushed the hair out of my eyes. "Are you okay, Princess?"

"I will be now, thanks to you." I rose to my feet, brushing off my bare knees. "I can never repay you."

"Actually, you can repay me," he replied as he rose to his feet, too, and I realized how high he towered over me. I wasn't sure that I had ever seen someone as tall as him.

"Okay. Are you going to tell me what this favor is or are you going to forever let it be a mystery?" I asked, remembering that he had kept mentioning this mysterious favor he wanted from me in exchange for rescuing me.

Based on how I felt when I looked at him, it was hard to imagine me saying no to anything he was about to ask of me.

"I need you to marry me."

"You can't be serious." I thought he was joking at first, but there was a look of seriousness behind his emerald green eyes as he stared back at me. "You are serious."

"I am more serious than I have ever been about anything in my life, Princess," he said matter-of-factly.

"This is quite a commitment you're asking of me," I murmured.

"It was quite a favor I did you," he replied pointedly. "But this is a long-term commitment."

I swallowed hard, my cheeks flushing at the thought. He was absolutely gorgeous. Stunning. If I could build a dream man, it would have been him.

But I also didn't like that he was asking me to marry him as a favor.

The only thing I really wanted in life was to marry for love. I didn't want to be forced into a marriage with anyone. And even though he was certainly nice to look at, he was trying to force me into a marriage, too—the same way the King and Queen who I had just escaped had.

"If I was going to be forced into a marriage, I may as well have stayed in the castle." Except I knew full well that I would have been happier with this stranger who stood before me than I ever would have been with Milos Santorini.

Still, why was he so insistent on a random stranger marrying him? Oh. Correction: why was he so insistent on a princess marrying him? I realized that I must have solved the mystery. This random stranger had helped me escape merely so he could marry a princess.

"Why do you wish to marry me?" I asked him, mostly curious about whether or not he would tell me the truth.

"If you marry me, Princess, you will make me a King." Well, at least he was honest, I supposed.

"Actually, you are incorrect in your assumptions," I informed him. "I am not yet a Queen. Marrying me will only make you a Prince." I paused, thinking about it. "Now that I have run away from the palace, I guess I will never actually get to be a Queen, so therefore, you would never have the opportunity to become King, either."

"Even though you've run away, you're still a Royal. My plans for us go bigger than Nocturne Island," he explained. "We can start our own kingdom. We'll build a fortress that's all ours on another island, and we will reign over it completely, without a care in the world—just you and me. There's another benefit of you marrying me," he added. "Once you are mine, then you belong to me. No one could ever force

you to marry anyone ever again. What do you say, Princess?"

He got down on one knee then. Staring up into my eyes, he took my hand in his. "Will you marry me?"

Every ounce of my being knew this wasn't a good idea. It would have been completely foolish of me to marry someone whose name I didn't even know, someone whose intentions couldn't have been entirely pure if he was asking me to do something so extreme for his sake.

And yet, I found myself drawn *to him for some reason.*

I wasn't sure what it was about this guy who stood before me, but there was this magnet-like energy, a force between us that just made me want to be with him. I wanted to marry him and have babies with him.

Did this mean that he was my mate? I was afraid that if I didn't agree to marry him, then I would never actually know.

So, even though I knew it was a foolish thing to do, I nodded. "Yes. I will marry you."

He beamed up at me and then stood up. "Perfect. We'll get married tonight."

"Tonight? How will I plan the wedding of my dreams?"

"A marriage is about the union of a man and woman, not about the wedding ceremony, isn't it, Princess?" I could hear the tone behind his voice; it challenged me.

"Under ordinary circumstances, I suppose so," I replied. "But nothing about this situation is what one would call ordinary."

"I'm going to be honest with you, Princess. When I broke into that castle with the intentions of rescuing you, I had one thing on my mind and one thing only—and that was becoming King. But now that I've met you, I would be lying to you if I told you I didn't want to marry you for who you are."

There was so much sincerity behind his voice that it was hard for me not to believe him.

*"So, what I'm asking you is to please marry me tonight."
There was a hopeful look in his emerald green eyes.*

"Okay," I agreed. "I'll marry you tonight." I paused for a moment and then asked, "Are you going to tell me your name now, at least?"

He smiled. "If I told you my name, there's no way in hell you would ever want to marry me."

"Why wouldn't I?" I asked him.

"Trust me. You wouldn't. I have quite a reputation. The Queen hates me."

"Then that's all the more reason for me to like you," I replied, a smile hitting my lips. "I'm not sure if you've figured this out about me yet, but I tend to like everything that my mother doesn't like."

"I know you're quite the rebel." He smiled down at me. "I have a feeling that you and I are going to get along really well, Princess. I can feel it in my bones. Together, we are going to become the most powerful Royals who will ever walk the paranormal realm."

Once the memory had finished playing through my eyes, so many realizations hit me. I glanced over at Kane again.

"I remember now. You always wanted to be King," I murmured. "This was your... your *dream*." Some guys dreamed of being teachers, and others dreamed of being police officers and firefighters. But, for hundreds of years, Kane had dreamt of being King.

Was I even special, or would he have chosen to become any princess's prince?

He nodded. "Yeah, it was a dream of mine."

"You've always been hungry for power." I swallowed hard, becoming slightly more upset by everything that I had just remembered about him. "So, that truly was the reason you helped me to escape that night—in exchange for becoming King."

Kane nodded. "It was."

"Wow." I just pursed my lips, unsure of what to make of all of this. "I'm not even sure what to think right now, honestly." I could feel the emotions building within me: confusion, betrayal, and, most of all, anger. I let out a little snort. "Well, I guess your dream came true, didn't it? You got exactly what you always wanted from me. You get to wear a crown and strut around this castle like you fucking own the place. I guess that, technically, you *do* own part of it."

"Raven, calm down. Please." Kane's eyes settled on mine. "That day, hundreds of years ago, has nothing to do with what we are currently going through."

"Really? It doesn't? Because the last time I checked, you were hungry for power then, and you're *still* hungry for power now. You haven't changed a bit."

"Back then, I didn't know the first thing about you. Now, I love you. I'm *in love* with you."

Aiden's words echoed through my mind:

"He's a narcissistic asshole. He doesn't love anyone but himself. He never has, and he never will. It doesn't matter that you're his mate or that you're carrying his child. He will never love you, Raven."

I met Kane's gaze. "Why didn't we get married that night? You were so insistent about wanting to get married that night, but it just never happened."

"Because I met a prophet in the woods. She showed me one of her visions. She told me that we couldn't get married yet—the timing wasn't right. She said we would both die if we got married back then. We had to wait for hundreds of years before we could ever be together." His green eyes lingered on mine. "So, I waited for you. I waited for hundreds of years before ever considering the possibility of marrying you again. I was patient."

"So, we just fell out of touch for hundreds of years while you were waiting?" Something about his story just wasn't adding up.

"There's a lot more to this, but I don't have to explain it to you right now, Raven. I just want you to know that I waited for you because I knew that you were different. I knew that you were my mate."

"And yet, you married Miriam," I replied quietly.

"Miriam was a mistake. I'm pretty sure that she put some sort of love spell on me," Kane insisted.

I opened my mouth to respond, but that was when I felt it: an excruciating pain that radiated through my core.

CHAPTER 17

I gasped loudly, touching my stomach.

"Raven, what's wrong? Are you okay?" Concern was written all over Kane's face.

I groaned out in pain, shaking my head. "No."

Something wasn't right. I could feel it. But I wasn't sure what was wrong, either.

"Is the baby coming?" Kane asked.

"I-I don't know." Hunched over, I managed to climb off the bed. When I looked at my white comforter, all I saw was crimson.

There was blood everywhere.

What was even happening?

I let out a bloodcurdling scream.

Kane stared at them, swallowing hard, before glancing back over at me. "The baby," he murmured.

I nodded.

At that moment, a feeling of weakness came over me. "I feel really lightheaded and dizzy. I think I need to see a doctor."

"I don't think there are any doctors on this island," Kane said quietly.

"Gloria. I need to see Gloria," I whispered.

Kane scooped me up into his arms, lifting me out of bed and carrying me out of the room. That was the last thing I remembered before everything went black.

* * *

"Do you think she's going to be okay?" I heard Kane asking.

"She will be just fine," Gloria said. "The spell I just put on the baby will calm him or her down... for now."

That was all it took to bring me to total alertness. My eyes fluttered open, and I glanced over at Gloria. "You put a spell on the baby?"

"Yes, I'm afraid that there was really no other option," Gloria said with a sigh. "I was able to determine, through a spell, that the baby became angry at you."

"*Angry* at me?" My eyebrows lifted questioningly. We were going to really butt heads if this baby was angry at me while it was still inside my womb.

"Yes. I'm afraid the baby was actually trying to kill you."

"Kill me? But I'm his mom. Or her mom." I paused. "Were you able to see its gender?"

Gloria shook her head. "No, I wasn't, Your Majesty."

"Oh." I was slightly disappointed by that. But mostly, I was confused by everything that had just happened. "I'm so confused. Why would the baby want to kill me?"

How in the world could a baby—*my* baby—want to kill

me? It didn't even know me yet, and already it hated me? What had I done to make it so angry at me? None of this made any sense.

"I'm really not sure, Your Majesty. To be frank, this is a rather… unique situation. In fact, I've never actually heard of this happening before. The only thing I *will* say is that this baby is strong—very, very strong. You need to take it easy. And if this happens again, then I think we should probably consider inducing labor."

"But we don't even know how far along I am. We don't know if the baby is even ready to come out yet," I insisted.

"This baby is a fighter. He or she will be okay. My concern is for you, Raven." Gloria's eyes met mine. "I'm afraid that if this happens again, your baby will kill you."

CHAPTER 18

*T*hat night, Kane and I decided to stay in my bedroom. He had the chef make me a grilled cheese sandwich made with equal parts sharp cheddar and mozzarella, my favorite comfort food from when I was a child, and we got lost in a marathon of *How I Met Your Mother.* Kane had never seen it before, and watching it made me feel sort of normal for once. Sort of... human.

Of course, I was anything *but* normal or human. The baby I was carrying had literally almost murdered me. It had been one of the scariest experiences of my life, right up there with the day Theo was murdered.

My mate had been killed, and now my baby was trying to kill *me*.

I felt so traumatized.

I really wished that all of my mates could have been there with me after the scare I'd had earlier, but I was glad that Kane was with me, at least. I couldn't imagine going through it completely alone.

Even though things had been rocky between us in the

past, he had proven tonight that he would be there for me always. He would be there when it counted, which was all that I could ask for.

For the first time since I had married him, it made me feel like I had made the right choice. I hadn't made a huge mistake, after all. I had chosen a King who did protect me when I needed to be protected.

"So, I was thinking," Kane said, turning to me as the episode we were watching came to an end. "This baby could be born any week now. We should probably discuss names, shouldn't we?"

"Oh. Yeah. Names." I touched my belly gently. What would we name this little monster that was growing in my stomach?

"I know we've thrown a few ideas around already, but we should probably give it some more thought," Kane went on. "We need to choose a good name. This baby is going to be the next King or Queen after our own reign. He or she needs a strong name—a powerful name. A name that's fit for the next ruler of the werewolves."

"I couldn't agree more." I gave it some thought. "For a girl, how about Elizabeth?"

Kane frowned. "That seems so cliché. It would make everyone think she was named after Queen Elizabeth."

I decided not to tell him that was where I had come up with the idea.

I scratched Catherine off my list.

"Anastasia," I suggested.

"Like the Grand Duchess of Russia?" Kane asked, wrinkling his nose.

"Actually, I was thinking of the character from *Fifty Shades of Grey*." I paused for a moment. "Isadora?"

His green eyes slid over to meet mine. "Can you really picture our daughter being named Isadora?"

"Good point." There weren't even any good nickname options for that one, unless she wanted to go by Dora, like the Nickelodeon show.

"Lydia," Kane suggested.

"After Queen Lydia, my biological mother? No thanks." Even though all I had were memories of the woman, I still blamed her for a lot of the things that had gone wrong in my life, like the fact that Milos Santorini had started a paranormal world war all because he had never given up hope of making a marriage with me happen. But he never would have had the idea in his mind to begin with if it weren't for the fact that Queen Lydia had promised it to him in the first place.

Yeah. There was no way in hell I was naming my baby after that woman. Over my dead body.

"Okay. I guess that one's out of the question."

I thought about it for a long moment. "Ella."

Kane considered it for a long moment before nodding. "Ella is nice. That's an option." He paused for a moment. "What about for a boy?"

"William," I said, a little too quickly.

"Like Prince William?" His eyebrows lifted as he glanced over at me.

I rolled my eyes. "There are just some names I associate with royals, what can I say?"

"No William, and before you suggest it, no Harry either."

"Michael. James. Edwin."

"Edwin?" Kane's eyebrows lifted questioningly.

I shrugged.

"Jason."

"Jason is *not* a royal-sounding name," I protested.

"Fair enough. Bartholomew."

I wrinkled my nose. "We are *not* naming our kid Bartholomew."

"Well, do you have any better ideas?" Kane challenged.

I thought about it for a long moment and then glanced over at him. "Theo."

"Theo? Seriously?" His green eyes met mine.

I nodded. "Yeah. It's a good name—a strong name. And it would be a good way for us to honor Theo, a way to keep his memory alive forever."

He shook his head in annoyance. "No. No way. We're not naming our kid after Theo."

"Why? Theo was my mate and a part of this pack. Doesn't he deserve to be honored in some sort of way?"

"You're still in love with him, aren't you?" Kane's green eyes just stared into mine accusingly.

"I'll always love Theo," I admitted quietly.

"I knew it. I fucking knew it." His eyes flashed with anger. "You know that you're *my* wife, right?"

"As if being your wife actually holds any meaning," I muttered under my breath.

"What are you getting at?" Kane asked.

"Miriam was your wife, too. That didn't stop you from murdering her," I pointed out.

"That has nothing to do with this conversation." His eyes darted away from mine.

It had everything to do with it. Clearly the title of "wife" meant nothing to him.

"Why did you kill her, Kane?" I pressed.

"That's a conversation for another day. Today, we're talking about Theo and the fact that you still love him even though he's dead. You realize that, right? Theo is dead and he's never coming back. But I'm here. You're my wife. I am the only one who you're supposed to be in love with. Not Theo," he spat.

Under ordinary circumstances, I would have said that he wasn't wrong. But the truth was that Theo wasn't the only one who I was still in love with. Every time I looked at Aiden, Rhys, and Colton, all I could think about was how I was madly in love with them, too. Even though I had thought that marrying Kane would change the way I felt about my other mates, the truth was that my feelings for them had only grown stronger—especially when he acted like this.

"I can't believe you still love Theo," he muttered under his breath.

Glancing over at him, I noticed for the first time that he was shaking—actually shaking—with anger.

"Kane, I don't understand why you're getting angry. Like you said, Theo is dead. You do realize you're getting jealous over a dead guy, right?"

"You're the one that's *making* me jealous," he said through gritted teeth.

"It's not my fault that you feel threatened by a dead guy," I said with a shrug.

"You do realize you want to name our son—*my* son— after the guy you loved, who just so happens to be my biggest enemy, don't you?" Kane shot back at me as he climbed out of my bed and slipped his shoes back on.

"Aren't you being a little dramatic?" I asked him.

"Nothing about the way I'm acting is dramatic. No one would want to name their son after their worst enemy, and it's pretty messed up that you would even suggest such a thing."

"I know that you and Theo didn't always see eye to eye, but was he really your worst enemy?" I wasn't trying to be insensitive or anything, but it had never seemed that way to me. They had managed to live in the Darken house together. It was for a very short time before Theo had been killed, but no fights or anything had broken up. They had seemed to be civil. At times, they even acted like they were *friends.* So, even though Theo had mentioned in the past, I supposed that, in a way, this whole "enemy" thing sort of caught me off-guard.

I had known that they were once enemies or rivals, but I had figured that they'd moved past all of that. Or at least, that was how it had seemed back when Theo was still alive.

"Yes, Raven, he was. There's a lot that went on between me and Theo that you don't know—a lot that you'll *never* know," Kane explained.

"Well, of course I won't know unless you tell me about it," I said pointedly.

"I don't feel like talking about it." He sighed. "I'm going back to my bedroom for the night."

"You're not going to stay with me?" Disappointment flooded my veins.

"No. You've put me in a bad mood now. In fact, you

made me want to be far away from you. Goodnight." As he slipped out of my room, closing the door loudly behind him, I buried my face in my pillow and began to cry.

So much for him protecting me. It looked like he wasn't actually the perfect mate, or the perfect King.

Really, it seemed like he was just a spiteful, jealous mate.

I wondered if he would try to kill me next, the way he had killed Miriam.

I supposed that it only made sense that our child, *his* child, had already tried to murder me.

* * *

I TRIED to sleep that night, but I found it difficult to. Fighting with Kane was the worst. It made me wonder, yet again, if I had made the wrong decision.

I thought about how I had made a mistake by breaking my other mates' hearts and changing the dynamics of our pack forever. Was it even possible for us to ever be as close as we once were? It sort of felt like they would never forgive me for choosing Kane.

I supposed that I didn't blame them, considering everything.

And that wasn't the only thing that kept me up that night. I also kept thinking of Theo and about the argument of naming our baby after him. I didn't think it was such an unreasonable request to name our child after my now deceased mate. And the truth was that it was something I *still* wanted to do, even if Kane didn't approve of it.

Even though a big part of me felt like we should name

our child something we agreed upon, I also wanted to go against his wishes and name our baby Theo, anyway. At the end of the day, I was Queen by blood and not through marriage. Didn't that mean that our baby's name should have ultimately been up to me?

Besides, it wasn't like Kane was all that reliable. Should he have even had a say in what we named our kid? As it was, there was a possibility that our kid was going to kill me, and he had gone back to the King Quarters, all due to a stupid argument. So much for how concerned he was about my safety. It almost seemed like he didn't care about me.

Sighing, I flicked the TV on and turned on the news.

There was video footage of the war. The bombs, which shots silver bullets for miles around, were going off, and there were fallen soldiers.

Watching it made me feel sick to my stomach. Instead of worrying about fighting with Kane every day, I needed to focus on how to stop this war. Too many lives were being lost. It made me feel hopeless, even though I knew that I was somehow going to be the one to ultimately end it.

Turning the TV back off, I laid in bed and sighed. I wasn't sure why, but I had a random urge to look out the window then.

Rising to my feet, I was relieved that I was no longer in any sort of pain; whatever damage the baby had caused to my body early had already healed up.

Glancing out the window, I stared up at the moon. It was full. It casted a golden glow over the garden below, unlike anything I had ever seen before. It looked like something out of a movie or something.

It felt like magic.

After a few moments, I spotted something out in the garden. It looked like a quick movement at first, a rustling in the bushes, but then I saw a wave of short black hair.

Someone was out there lurking in the rural garden, and I was pretty sure that I had a good idea of who that someone was.

Milos Santorini.

Pulling a hoodie on over my head, I opened my dresser drawer and grabbed the gun. My hand trembled as I held it. Kane had put the gun in my drawer when we had first moved into the castle, but I had never thought I would actually need to *use it.* One of my mates was almost always with me.

Except for right now, when I felt like I needed them the most.

But after seeing who I could have only assumed was Milos creeping around outside, I knew I had no choice *but* to use it. And knowing that I was holding the weapon that would kill him made me feel an array of emotions. Nervousness. Fear. Anxiety.

But most of all? *Power.* I held the power to end his life in my right hand.

I knew how to use a gun, of course. Colton had taught me well in my Weaponry class during my first year at Werewolf Academy. But knowing how to use a gun and *actually* using a gun were two entirely different things.

As I slipped into my boots and snuck out of my bedroom quarters, I couldn't help but feel relieved that

Kane had decided not to spend the night with me. The last thing I needed was for him to talk me out of going outside. He would have probably gone in my place, and that wasn't what I wanted. I wanted to be the one to kill Milos, as crazy as it may have sounded.

So, I crept down the hallway, being sure to move as quietly as possible, afraid of waking Kane or my friends up.

The truth was that I wanted to end this whole thing once and for all, entirely on my own. I didn't want to have to involve any of them if I didn't need to.

Plus, when it came down to it, this whole thing was between me and Milos. It had *always* been between me and Milos. I didn't want my friends to end up getting hurt in the crossfire if it could have been avoided.

I would have never been able to live with myself if one of them get caught up in this mess and died—ultimately, because of me.

Glancing around the garden, I held the gun at my side. I was nervous. I had never killed anyone before, but it was time to end the game he had started. I was getting really freaking sick and tired of playing.

I debated calling him out, but I also didn't want to blow up my spot. I knew that my odds of actually killing him were much better if I caught him off-guard.

Then again, he was probably already completely aware that I was out here looking for him. That was probably why he was so difficult to find. He was probably hiding from me, waiting to capture me and kidnap me again.

No matter what happened, I wouldn't let him kidnap me. Not now, or ever.

I would finish him in that garden.

I held my breath as I turned every corner, hoping to find him and actually kill him. My heart pounded against my chest with every move I made, and sure enough, I didn't see him anywhere.

I scanned every inch of the garden, and after what felt like *for*-freaking-*ever* looking for him, I finally gave up.

Feeling completely defeated, I turned to head back to the castle when a familiar voice said, "Raven, wait."

I froze.

There was no way. No freaking way.

And yet, when I turned, it was him who stared back at me.

It wasn't Milos.

It was Theo.

CHAPTER 19

*H*is striking blue eyes locked on mine as he stepped out from behind one of the rose bushes.

"T-Theo?" I could barely speak as I stared back at him.

My heart pounded against my chest. How was this even *possible*? There was no way that he could have been standing there in front of me right now, and yet... he was.

I had forgotten had gorgeous he was. Aside from some extra facial scruff, he hadn't changed at all since the day he had died.

Except, he hadn't died, if he was standing right there in front of me.

I pinched myself, wondering if I was lost inside one of my dreams. I'd had so many of Theo being alive and seeing him again since I had seen his body lying there.

This felt like it was the realest, by far.

It hurt when I pinched myself. I definitely was not dreaming. He was really here, standing right in front of me. There was no denying it. Theo freaking Rossi was standing there in the flesh.

But how?

"You're alive?" I asked.

Theo nodded.

A million feelings began to swarm through me as I tried to wrap my head around the fact that he was here.

Confusion. I had seen his dead body. How could this have been possible when I had seen him lying there in his coffin? I had watched that coffin be lowered into the ground. I had experienced the pain of losing him forever. I had felt his absence. So, how could he have been standing here in front of me?

Relief. He was here. He was really here. I had wished for this to happen so many times in the past, and it was actually happening. My wishes had come true.

Anger? Maybe anger. Was this all some sort of joke? Had I really just been in the middle of the world's biggest prank? Why would he have bamboozled me like that? If it was a prank, did he realize how much pain it had caused me?

There was another possibility...

Was he a ghost?

I reached out to touch his cheek. When my fingertips brushed against his warm skin, I gasped.

"Oh my god." I covered my mouth with my hands. "I'm not losing it. You really *are* here right now. You're alive. How can you be alive?"

"Raven, shh," he whispered into my ear. "You have to be quiet. I'm not even supposed to be here right now."

"W-what do you mean?" My heart pounded against my chest.

"I only came here to try to steal a glimpse of you. I wasn't supposed to talk to you. It was a rule I made for myself, but I couldn't just let you go back to the castle without saying something to you." His blue eyes poured into mine. "If he knew I was here, he would be so pissed at me. Me being here isn't a part of the plan."

I blinked. "What plan?"

There was a plan? A plan that he had completely avoided informing me about until right now.

"I faked my own death, Raven," Theo whispered.

"But... why? Why would you do that to me?" I swallowed hard.

"I can't tell you the reason. Not yet."

"No. I need to know the reason you would do this to me. How could you do that to me? I loved you, Theo—I *still* love you. Why would you make me believe you were dead?" I tried to swallow the lump of pain that had lodged itself in my throat.

"It's the hardest thing I've ever done, but you should know that it killed me, too. Every day, it's been killing me. That's why I had to see you again." His blue eyes didn't stray away from mine as he spoke.

"But none of this even makes sense. How could you have faked your death when I *felt* you die? When our mate bond broke, I could feel it: physically, emotionally, mentally—everything. When you died, it felt like a part of me died, too." I shook my head, trying to make sense of all of this. "How did I feel it if you never even died at all?"

"It was magic, Raven. We had a witch sever the tie

between us," Theo explained. "She broke the mate bond, so it felt like I died." He swallowed hard. "I felt it, too. You weren't the only one. The physical pain of our severed mate bond is still something I live with to this day." He paused for a moment, "It feels like my heart is continuously broken every day."

"Me, too," I whispered. "But I'm still confused. I saw your dead body. We *buried* your dead body," I insisted. "There was no way you could have faked any of that."

Had he somehow unburied himself and climbed out of his coffin? It didn't even add up. It's not like we were vampires, who could physically do that if they wanted to. But we needed food and water to live. Unless he climbed out of his grave right away...

"It was magic, Raven. We used magic to create a replica of my body to make everyone believe I was dead."

"You keep saying 'we'. Who is 'we'?" I asked him.

His eyes locked on mine. "I can't tell you that. I'm sworn to secrecy."

"Was it the rest of the Darken who helped you fake your own death?" I already felt so much betrayal from Theo for doing this to me. But I would have felt even more betrayed if my other pack members... my other mates... had known all along that Theo was alive and kept it from me.

"No, it wasn't them. And you have to promise me that you won't tell them that you saw me tonight, or it will defeat the purpose of *all* this."

"How will it defeat the purpose?" I asked him.

"Just promise me you won't say a word to any of the

others, Raven. Please." There was a serious look in Theo's eyes.

"I promise, but I need you tell me why you did this." I shot him a pleading look.

"I wish I could tell you everything, but I can't. Not yet, anyway. I know it's really confusing right now, but it will all make sense in the end." There was a sincerity in his tone that I couldn't ignore. But it didn't matter how genuine it seemed like he was being; it didn't change the fact that he had been gone for nearly six months. Six months that we could never get back.

It also didn't change the fact that during that time, I had married Theo's enemy. I hadn't just married him; I had made him King of the wolves—something I was fairly certain I wouldn't have done if Theo had been alive.

Well, if I had known he was alive, that was. I was pretty sure that if I had known, he was the one who I would have chosen to be my King.

And now that I knew he was alive, I couldn't help but want to put the blame on him.

"Why would you do this?" I finally asked. "Why would you fake your own death?"

Why would you leave me on purpose? I couldn't bring myself to ask him that one. Partly because I knew that I couldn't speak the words out loud without breaking down, and also because I was too afraid to know what the answer was.

"I wish I could tell you everything right now, but I can't. I don't have enough time. I have to leave soon. I've already stayed for too long." His blue eyes met mine, and he wrapped his arms around me. "I just had to see you, Raven. I've missed you more than you could ever know."

I just stared at him. There were a million questions floating around inside my mind, so many things I wanted to ask him. But if what he was saying was true... *if* he really didn't have enough time to stay here much longer, I didn't want to ruin what little time we had left together.

I wasn't sure if I would ever see him again, or how long it would be before I would. All I knew was that I wished that I could stay in this moment forever.

"I've missed you, too," I finally replied as I laid my head against his shoulder, giving into his embrace.

That was when I felt it: the baby in my stomach suddenly began to go crazy again, kicking with so much fierceness.

But for some reason, I could tell that it had calmed down; it no longer wanted to kill me. It was just... excited. I wasn't sure how I knew that, but I did.

Was it possible that the baby felt my own excitement? Was it able to tell that I was with the one who I loved, the one who I really wanted to be with?

After a few moments, we pulled away from one another and his blue eyes locked on mine. "You're pregnant," he whispered.

"How did you know?" I asked.

"I can hear it kicking." His hands fell to my stomach.

It was the first time anyone besides Kane had touched my belly.

"How far along are you?" he asked.

"Gloria couldn't tell for sure. She says determining the length of a pregnancy for an Ancient works differently than it does for other werewolves. There's no expected time frame like a typical werewolf pregnancy or even a human pregnancy. It's just whenever the baby is ready to be born. So, technically, it could happen any day now."

"I know. Ancient werewolf babies are complex." Removing his hands from my stomach, Theo stared deep into my eyes. "I love you, Raven. I promise this is all going to make sense one day. And when it does... I'll be back for you." His deep blue eyes pierced through me, straight into my soul. "I'll come back to claim what's mine."

"Theo, I already made a choice," I replied quietly. "I-I married Kane."

Even *if* I thought it was a mistake a lot of days, that didn't mean that it hadn't happened. It also didn't mean I could do anything to change it.

"I know."

"You do?"

"It's been all over the news. Everyone in our world knows." His eyes didn't move away from mine. "What I'm not sure about is why you had to choose him. Of all of the Darken, my worst enemy?"

I swallowed hard. "It's complicated."

"It doesn't seem that complicated to me. You chose Kane, the guy who has betrayed me numerous times. I'm not sure what could be so complicated about it."

"If you had been here, then maybe I wouldn't have had to marry your enemy," I snapped at him. "Maybe I would have married you instead. In fact, I can say pretty confidently that I *would* have married you. You are the one who I would have chosen. You're the one who chose to fake your own death."

"It wasn't my idea to fake my own death." There was a genuine look behind his eyes. "It was his idea."

"Whose idea was it, Theo? You're not making any sense." I just stared back at him, completely confused by everything he was saying.

"I have to go, Raven." Leaning in closer to me then, his lips came crashing down on mine.

Wrapping my arms around his neck, I pulled him in closer to me, deepening the kiss.

His mouth lingered on mine longer than it normally did when he kissed me. It was as if he was studying it to remember it for later. That made me fear how long it would be before we would see each other again... how long before we would kiss one another again.

When I glanced up at the night sky, that was when I saw it.

Shooting stars were falling down all around us, the same way they had the first time we had ever kissed on Nocturne Island.

I wasn't entirely sure what that meant, but I did know one thing was for sure.

It had to have meant something.

CHAPTER 20

*E*ntering the castle, I couldn't hide the giddiness that had taken over.

Theo was alive. He was *actually* alive.

Even though he'd had to leave me again for now, I was confident that this wasn't forever. I believed him when he'd said that one day, all of this would make sense.

I was sort of angry at myself for promising not to tell the other Darken members. It was them who I wanted to break the good news to most.

Theo hadn't said I couldn't tell Maddie or Vince, though. So, that was exactly where I was headed.

I had just rounded the corner to head up the stairs that led to my bedroom when I felt it: the faint feeling that came over me.

I thought I could fight it, but I could feel myself growing weak in the knees.

At first, I thought that the baby was trying to hurt me again, but I quickly realized that it wasn't that. No, this time, it had nothing to do with the pregnancy.

It had been such a long time since I had felt this way before, but I knew exactly what had triggered it.

Theo's kiss.

Our mate bond had been reignited. And that was the best thing that had happened to me in a long time. That was all I could think about before my eyes fluttered shut and everything went black.

* * *

WHEN I CAME to alertness again, my head was throbbing.

The last thing I remembered was kissing Theo in the garden and then passing out.

I knew that I had probably hit my head on the stone floor and gotten some type of head injury or something. I was relieved that I was a werewolf, so whatever it was would heal up fast.

As I opened my eyes and took in my surroundings, I was surprised to find that I was no longer laying on the stone floor.

I was in what looked like a wooden shed or barn, and my arms and legs were bound together with rope, and there was tape over my mouth.

What the actual fuck.

How in the world had I even gotten here?

It took a moment for me to realize that Milos Santorini must have found me in the hallway and then moved me here.

I wasn't sure what he was planning, but honestly? I was ready to just get this all over with already. We needed to just face each other and get this over with already. I wanted to believe that I was strong enough to kill him since I had managed to successfully kill Iris. I was tired from running from him, and even more tired of him kidnapping me.

A few moments later, I heard the sound of the door opening, and light streamed in through the room. It was dark, so at first all I saw was the figure that stood before me. He was wearing a black hooded sweatshirt, black pants, and a black mask covering everything but his eyes.

As he flicked on a light in the barn or whatever we were in, I quickly realized that those weren't Milos Santorini's eyes.

Milos had black eyes, but these eyes were much lighter in color. The lighting was dim, so I couldn't make out the exact color, but they weren't black.

I realized that whoever stood before me was also much shorter than Milos was. So short, in fact, that I began to wonder if it was a man or a woman.

Somehow, being kidnapped had actually been less scary when I had thought that Milos was the one who had kidnapped me. Now that I didn't know who had kidnapped me, I suddenly felt on edge.

"Oh, you're awake," a familiar female voice said.

As she pulled her mask off, I would have gasped if my mouth wasn't taped shut.

Queen Lydia stood before me.

I thought back to the dream I'd had of Milos when he had told me that my mother wasn't actually dead.

Apparently, I was right. That dream *had* been real... and he had been right.

The Queen stood before me, staring at me through

175

narrowed eyes. "I'll remove the tape from your mouth, as long as you promise not to scream. That's the entire reason I taped it shut to begin with—so that you won't tip anyone off about your whereabouts. If you scream, I will put the tape back—and leave you here for days with no food," she threatened. "I know you're with child. I'm sure the last thing you want is to go without eating. You starving means the baby will starve, and if I were you, I wouldn't want a werewolf baby to starve while inside of me. I have a feeling it wouldn't be pretty."

Wow, she was wicked.

"Do you agree not to scream?" Queen Lydia asked.

I nodded.

She ripped the tape off of my mouth, not even being the slightest bit gentle.

Then she slapped me across the cheek.

I flinched.

"That," she said, "is for running away. You never should have run away from me, Fallyn. You ruined *everything.*"

"Everything? Like your whole grand scheme to force me to marry someone who I didn't love?" I pressed, not even bothering to explain to her that I didn't remember much about my old life except for the few visions that I'd had. Though there had been very few visions, they were important ones, at least.

"Who cares about love? Child, you have it all wrong. What you need to worry about is *power*. Power is what I wanted for you, Fallyn. If you had married Milos Santorini, you would have become the most powerful Queen in the paranormal world. But instead, the vampires rose to power because you ran from the perfect future that I had planned for you—all because you thought *love* was important." She looked completely disgusted by the fact that anyone could value love over power.

"First of all, my name is no longer Fallyn. I go by Raven now," I informed her.

"Oh, please. You're being absolutely ridiculous. I named you Fallyn. That's your name." She rolled her eyes at me.

"Second of all, it's nice to see you, too, *Mother*," I said. "You know, I always wondered if we ever met again someday if you would regret what happened between us."

"Me? You're the one who ran off in the middle of the night. How did you even escape from me that night?" she asked me. "I know that it must have been an invisibility spell, but I know that you knew nothing about your magical abilities at all, let alone how to use dark magic. I've always suspected that someone helped you to escape. It was those Gallagher's, wasn't it?" She narrowed her eyes at me.

"No. It wasn't," I replied. The truth was that I still didn't know how my parents had come to adopt me. "It was Kane Romero, the guy who I just married. The guy who I just made King."

"You've made Kane Romero King?" Queen Lydia looked completely shocked by this news.

"I would have thought that you would have heard about this already. The news of our marriage has broken out all over." Truthfully, I was shocked that she'd had no idea.

"I thought that Kane Romero was killed by the virus. He's still alive?" My mother asked.

"Yeah. I'm not sure why you're so surprised. I'd heard that you died because of the virus, too. Or was it that the vampires murdered you when they ambushed the castle? To be honest, I've lost track of all the ways you supposedly died, and yet *you're* still here," I said pointedly.

"Oh, that vampire ambush." Queen Lydia shook her head at the memory and let out a little laugh. "I'm the one who arranged that."

"You did?" I just stared back at her, completely confused as to why she would have wanted the vampires to attack the castle.

"Yes, well, I had to figure out *some* way to get rid of your father," she explained. "I'm sure you already know by now that I never loved him. I only ever married him for the power. But he was very controlling. He wasn't a good man. I was about to leave him when I fell pregnant with you, and then the curse was put on the island that made us werewolves. Once you were gone, I knew that I didn't want to spend the rest of my life with him, so I did what I had to do. I faked my own death to let the rest of the paranormal world believe I was dead. I've spent most of my life vacationing in the human world, but I recently caught wind of the fact that you returned to Nocturne Island. That's when I sent Sarah to Werewolf Academy."

Sarah had been my lady's maid back when I was Princess. She had appeared in my visions and then I later noticed her at Werewolf Academy, though she had gone by the name Lydia. Sarah had been Maddie's roommate.

"That's why she was there? Because you sent her?" I

wasn't sure what my mother had been hoping to accomplish.

The Queen nodded. "I was far too old to pass as a student, and I had stayed in touch with Sarah over the years. She was the only one besides me who knew you. I had to know if this Raven Gallagher I heard about was Fallyn—my Fallyn. Sarah was able to confirm that it was, in fact, you."

"Who told you I was there?" I asked her with wide eyes.

"Headmaster Black."

A weird feeling filled the pit of my stomach. I had already known that Headmaster Black wasn't a good guy. If he had been a good guy, he wouldn't have killed Jessica Davis, Milos Santorini's daughter. But I got the feeling that he was even worse than we had ever dreamed him to be.

"Don't blame Headmaster Black, of course. He isn't a bad guy."

I suppressed an eye roll. Of course she should say he wasn't a bad guy, considering *she* wasn't one of the good guys herself.

"Headmaster Black was good friends with those Gallagher people. They had always spoken about their daughter, but they always failed to produce a photograph of you. He thought this was strange, but it became even stranger when they inquired about Milos Santorini's whereabouts and started asking question about me."

"Questions about you?" My eyebrows rose questioningly.

"Yes. Apparently, they had caught wind of the fact that

I might have still been alive. I'm still not sure who might have told them." She shrugged. "Anyway, they seemed… worried. They thought Milos Santorini was trying to find out what town they lived in. I have no doubt that this is true. As you probably know by now, Milos Santorini is a bit obsessed with you."

"No thanks to you." I rolled my eyes at her.

"No thanks to yourself, either. Failing to follow through on an arranged marriage is sure to disappoint your potential suitor." She paused for a moment and then continued. "Anyway, your parents asked if Headmaster Black could guarantee you protection at Werewolf Academy. This seemed sort of out of sorts, even for them. Your parents had obviously been powerful werewolves from a very strong pack, but Headmaster Black began to piece the puzzle together on his own. The reason they had never produced a photo of you, the reason why you didn't even have a birth record… It all began to make sense. He was pretty sure that they were keeping you hidden. But he wasn't able to confirm it himself, since he had never actually met you. That was when we sent Sarah to Werewolf Academy, to figure out, once and for all, if you were Fallyn or not."

"Wow." It was crazy to think that all of this had been going on behind the scenes. Here I had just been trying to get through my courses at Werewolf Academy and become the most powerful werewolf I could be, and Headmaster Black had been talking to Queen Lydia about me this entire time.

I didn't think it was possible for me to trust that man less than I already had, but I did.

"I have a question," I said quietly. "I recently learned that my parents weren't killed by Milos Santorini."

"That's correct," she replied matter-of-factly. "Headmaster Black knew from the get-go that it hadn't actually been Milos."

Headmaster Black's words echoed through my mind then:

"Your adoptive parents had a lot of enemies in high places, Miss Gallagher. The truth is that it could have been just about anyone."

He had said those words when we had been talking about who might have tried to shoot Theo, and he had seemed almost confident that it hadn't been Milos Santorini. Was that because Headmaster Black had actually known who had killed my parents? Had he really known the truth about who seemed to want to kill all of the people who I loved so dearly?

I knew it was probably a longshot, but I found myself asking, "Did Headmaster Black ever mention who he thought might have really killed them?"

"No, but he didn't have to. I already know."

I just stared back at her, completely shocked. "Who was it?"

A grin tugged at her lips. "It was me, Fallyn."

CHAPTER 21

I just stared back at Queen Lydia, feeling completely disgusted with her. "*You're* the one who killed my parents?"

Here, I had mistakenly thought that it was Milos Santorini for so long—for literally years. When I had found out that it wasn't him, I had wondered who could have possibly wanted my adoptive parents to die.

My biological mother never would have crossed my mind, considering I hadn't even known that she was alive. But learning that it was her who had done made me feel physically sick.

Why would she have done this? *How* could she have done this?

"Oh, don't act so surprised. Anyone in my shoes would have done the same thing." She rolled her eyes at me. "Do you realize how it felt for me to learn that two powerful werewolves were raising the daughter I had given birth to? That they had wiped away all of your memories so that you wouldn't remember me or the life that they were trying to protect you from—even though it meant erasing your memories of *me*? What they did was wrong—extremely wrong."

"How did you even know that they did any of that?" I asked her with raised eyebrows.

"After Headmaster Black began to suspect that the Gallagher's had taken you under their wing, I had to investigate. I went to your town, and I followed you around. I followed you to the supermarket one day, and I even waved to you. You didn't even recognize me. That was the moment that I knew they had swiped your memories. So, I went to visit a very good witch, and she showed me a vision. It confirmed everything that I had thought to be true."

Queen Lydia reached out and touched me then.

A scene began to play out before me then, and I realized that she was transferring this witch's vision to me.

I WATCHED *as my parents stood talking to someone. At first, all I could see was their backs, but then the vision shifted, and I could see all four of their faces.*

Kane stood before my parents. "I heard that the two of you recently lost a son."

"Yeah, he was murdered by the vampires," my adoptive father explained.

"How could they kill a poor innocent werewolf child?" My mom swallowed hard. She was shaking, and I was pretty sure she was fighting the urge to cry.

My mother had never been one to cry in front of anyone.

She always put on a brave face, even during her darkest times. This had clearly been one of them.

"There's this myth that says that sacrificing a werewolf for their blood will make a vampire stronger," my father explained. "So, they sacrificed him. They drank all of his blood —every drop. They murdered our son, all for their own selfish gain."

"I'm so terribly sorry for your loss," Kane said. "I want to offer you my sincerest, deepest condolences."

"Thank you." My mom offered him a smile.

"What if I told you guys that I can help you get back at the vampires?" Kane asked.

"How could we do that?" My father asked.

"Well, it involves... adopting... a child. An older child. A teenager, actually. She's sixteen years old, and obviously she won't get any older. Would you be open to that?"

"We love children," my mom replied with a nod.

"What if I told you that I need you to adopt her on a long-term basis?" Kane asked.

"A long-term basis?" My dad looked confused.

"I know this all is going to sound a little... strange. The werewolf in question is Princess Fallyn."

"The Princess Fallyn who's next in line to be Queen?" My mom's eyes widened.

"That would be the one."

"Why would she need us to adopt her?" My dad asked. "She has parents of her own—ones who can offer her far more than we can."

"We could give a child a great life, but she is a Princess," my mom agreed with a nod. "I doubt she would want us to adopt her.

"Well, that's the thing. Princess Fallyn wouldn't actually know you're adopting her," Kane explained.

"How would she not know?" My dad asked.

"We would wipe away all of the memories that she currently has. I know it sounds extreme, but here's the thing. Her life is in very grave danger. I need you guys to protect her for me. She isn't safe here. She will never be safe here. Nocturne Island is dangerous for Fallyn."

"You mean, Queen Lydia is dangerous for Fallyn," my adoptive mother corrected him.

"That's right. How did you know?" Kane's eyes widened.

"I've heard... stories. One of the stories was that Queen Lydia wants to kill her own daughter. I thought it was just a story, but based on what you're telling us, it sounds like it could be true."

"It is true," Kane replied with a nod. "You see, the problem is that Queen Lydia will stop at nothing to make sure that Fallyn marries Milos Santorini."

"I've heard that he's ruthless. Savage." My mom looked horrified at the idea.

"You're not wrong about that, either. Fallyn wants nothing to do with the marriage. She doesn't love Milos. Who could love such a monster? He's not just a monster. He's a murderer—just like the vampires who killed your son. You wouldn't want her to have to end up in the wrong hands, would you?"

"Of course not," my mother agreed.

"Me either," Kane agreed. "The problem is that Queen Lydia still wants Fallyn to proceed with the marriage. I'm pretty sure that the Queen will even kill Princess Fallyn if she doesn't go through with the marriage, which was set to take place last night. Fortunately, I helped Fallyn escape. Here's the thing.

You're probably wondering why I am so invested in this. Well, Fallyn is the girl who I love, and she loves me. She's already agreed to spend the rest of her life with me, but that can't happen right now. It isn't safe right now. I need you guys to keep her safe for me."

"Of course. We'll do anything we can do to help," my adoptive father agreed with a nod.

"I want you to take her to a witch who lives in New York. Her name is Shonda. She will erase all of her memories of this life—of being Princess Fallyn and, most importantly, of Nocturne Island. If we don't get rid of those memories, there's a good chance that she'll try to come back. She can't do that. She has to forget about Nocturne Island, about her royal upbringing, and even about me."

"Why do you want her to forget you when you're so in love with one another?" My mom sounded sort of skeptical.

"Because now isn't the time for us to be together. I will come back for her when she's ready, but that won't be for a very long time," Kane replied. "I need you to wipe her memories away now and every so often. About every sixteen years or so, wipe her memories away and move to a new location. A new town, a new school, a new life. Please. I'm begging you." There was a pleading look in his eyes.

"Of course, Kane. We will raise her as if she was our own daughter," my adoptive father replied.

"Over and over again," my mom agreed with a nod.

"We'll do anything to avenge our son's death," my adoptive father added. "We will do whatever it takes you to help you overthrow them."

"Thank you. This means so much to me. One day, I will marry that girl—when the timing is right. She will become

Queen, and I will become King. And then I will make sure that the vampires are overthrown. I will make sure that they pay for what they did to your son. I promise you that."

"We'll take good care of her," my mother promised.

"And we'll be in touch," my adoptive father added.

"Good." Kane shot them a smile that made me want to punch him in the face.

THE MEMORY STOPPED JUST AS QUICKLY as it had begun, and I was left feeling sick to my stomach.

Wow.

Kane had done the best thing he could have done for me… in a way. He had protected me from the paranormal realm, from the werewolves, and from Queen Lydia. He had saved me from marrying Milos Santorini. And he had placed me into the care of my adoptive parents, who I would forever be grateful to know.

But he had done all of it for his own selfish gain. He had manipulated my poor, innocent adoptive parents into taking care of me, giving them hopes of helping them avenge the murder of their son.

I couldn't believe that my adoptive parents had even given birth to a child of their own, a child long before me.

They must have been in so much pain when they had agreed to help Kane keep me protected, and the pain that they'd experienced must have never gone away for them to continue to keep me protected for such a long time.

I was going to assume that, until the day they both had died, they had still wanted to avenge their biological son's death.

It made me feel so sad for them. And so angry at Kane for manipulating them the way he had, all so he could marry me in the end.

All because he wanted the power that came with being King.

What Kane had done was completely disgusting. And it was even more upsetting to know that this monster was the father of my baby.

What if my baby grew up to be like him? That was the absolute last thing I wanted, but I couldn't allow myself to forget that this baby was half him.

Half monster.

"So. That was intense, wasn't it?" Queen Lydia asked, interrupting my thoughts.

"To say the least," I muttered under my breath.

I hated Kane for what he had done. I hated him for using his manipulation tactics and trickery on my parents.

But I hated Queen Lydia even *more* for murdering my parents.

"What do you want from me, Lydia?"

"Actually, it's *Mother* to you," she said, a cold look in her eyes.

I ignored her. "Why did you kidnap me? What was the point?"

"I heard that you were with child." Her eyes met mine. "I want your baby, Raven."

I glared at her. "Over my dead body."

"I would think twice before you tell me 'no', brat." Queen Lydia's eyes met mine. "Guess who I happened to find out in the forest today?" She leaned in closer, showing me a picture on her cell phone.

I stared at Rhys, Colton, and Aiden. All three of them were laying in what looked like a pile of dirt. "What have you done to them?"

"They're in a hole in the ground right now. The cool thing about this little trap I've set up is that if they try to climb out, the sensors will trigger silver bullets to be shot off every so often." She shot me a wicked grin. "Hope they enjoy staying put."

I felt sick to my stomach. "Let them go."

"Gladly... in exchange for your baby."

"I'm not giving you my baby," I replied.

"If I was you, I would think again. Eventually, the Darken pack is going to try to climb their way out of that. They're bound to get hungry at some point. And if one of those guns happens to go off... Well, I would hate to think of what would happen to them." She glanced over at me. "We know all too well what happens when a silver bullet comes to close to a werewolf's heart, don't we now?"

My heart pounded against my chest. "It was *you* who shot Theo years ago on the Werewolf Academy campus?"

"Yeah. I know, that was something else that Milos got the blame for. But I set it up that way. I used magic to make myself look like him to trick you all into thinking it was me," she replied with a wicked laugh. "One thing you should probably know by now is that you can never outsmart a Queen." She winked at me.

I swallowed hard, feeling the tears flood my eyes. They were tears of anger. I hated this woman more than I ever thought myself capable of hating anyone.

The worst part about it all was that I wasn't even sure how much I could really hate Milos for anymore. It wasn't that I believed that he was good because he wasn't—that much I already knew, for sure. But so many things that I had thought he was behind were actually my mother's doing.

"So, what's it going to be? Are you going to hand your baby over to me or are you going to let your mates die?"

"Why do you even want my child?" I asked her then.

"I messed up with you. I want a second chance—a do-over." My mother stared down at my stomach. "I want the opportunity to raise the perfect future King or Queen."

"*I* am the Queen." I swallowed hard. "What if we can compromise? What if I allow you to be a part of your grandchild's life, if you let my mates go?"

"That simply isn't enough. I want to raise the baby as my own." Her eyes met mine. "You owe that to me, Fallyn. You ran away from me when you were far too young."

"I was nearly eighteen, Mother. It was time for me to leave the nest soon, anyway."

"You were never meant to leave. You were meant to marry Milos Santorini and become the most powerful Queen in the world. You, my dear, were too stubborn. My intentions are to raise this child to be the most powerful King there is."

"Or Queen. We don't know the gender yet," I informed her.

"It's a boy, darling. I am able to read baby genders, and your child's energy is completely masculine."

I had my doubts about what she was saying. "Fine. How's this? You let me go, and you let my mates go. Once the baby is born, I will hand him over to you."

And, in the meantime, I would try to come up with a

plan. I just needed to make sure that my mates were released before it was too late.

"You're lying, Fallyn. I can tell that you're lying. You don't actually want this," Queen Lydia said.

"I'm really not lying," I insisted, forcing a smile. "I would love to see him be raised by someone as lovely as you. You'll just be taking him off my hands."

"I don't believe you." She shrugged. "You should probably work on your lying skills. It's time for me to go check on your mates. We'll see if they're still alive, I suppose. In the meantime, you can sit here and think about what you need to do."

She turned to head out of the barn door, but then she turned to face me. "I nearly forgot to tape your mouth shut."

Ripping some tape off of the roll, she placed it over my mouth again.

Then, she closed the door to the barn again, leaving me in complete and total darkness.

CHAPTER 22

 s I stared into the darkness, I could feel my anger building with every minute that passed.

Who did Queen Lydia think she was to believe she was entitled to my baby? My son, possibly.

It just made me feel completely disgusted.

What disgusted me just as much was the fact that Kane hadn't even figured out that I was gone yet. He was probably still sleeping peacefully in the King's Quarters, completely unaware that I wasn't in my Queen's Quarters.

I made a decision then. I no longer wanted to be with him. Once I got back to the castle, I was going to end the marriage.

I wasn't sure how he was going to respond to that. But I would worry about that later. Right now, I needed to figure out how the hell I was going to get out of here.

I tried to use my magic.

I thought about how I wanted the rope around my wrists to break. I tried to do every type of magic I could think of to break the rope and open the door.

But nothing I did seemed to work. I figured out then that my mother must have put a block up to prevent me from using my magic within the confines of the barn.

It figured that she would do that. Anything she could do to prevent me from escaping from her hell.

I supposed that it shouldn't have surprised me. My last memory of Queen Lydia was her holding me prisoner in her tower, and now she was holding me prisoner in this barn.

That seemed to be how our relationship seemed to go.

Well, I had gotten away from her once.

I would figure out a way to do it again.

* * *

I WASN'T sure how much time had passed. I saw the sun rise and set again. I was at least one day into this prison, and I still hadn't figured out how the hell I was going to get out of it.

All I knew was that, once I did, there was going to be some serious hell to pay.

I was tired and hungry. I knew the baby was hungry, too.

It surprised me that the baby hadn't tried to kill me again. If it was going to hate me, it should have been hating me for not feeding it.

I was sure that it was just a matter of time.

I didn't want to think negatively, but I had a feeling that we were going to die out here.

I was beginning to feel really angry at Kane for not figuring out my whereabouts by now. I didn't know how far away I was from the castle, but Nocturne Island wasn't *that* big. He should have sent out a search party for me by now.

Then again, for all I knew, maybe there *was* a search party out there looking for me. Maybe Queen Lydia had just kept me so well-hidden that no search party could even find me. I was pretty sure that she knew this island better than most of us did.

I had always tried to stay optimistic, but honestly? I was beginning to lose hope.

THREE MORE DAYS PASSED, and I didn't think I was going to live much longer unless I drank water or ate something.

I could feel myself getting weaker every day.

This wasn't how a werewolf pregnancy was supposed to go.

I was surprised when I heard the sound of the barn door open that night. It was dark out, but I knew that it could have only been Lydia.

But to my surprise, there was a male figure who stood in the doorway. He was wearing a hooded sweatshirt, so I didn't see his face at first.

But when he approached me, my heart pounded against my chest.

"Relax, Raven. Your heart is beating like a humming-bird. I'm not going to hurt you," he said, as his black eyes locked on mine. "I've actually come to rescue you."

CHAPTER 23

*A*s Milos Santorini peeled the tape off of my mouth, his eyes locked on mine. "You seem so timid around me."

"Why would you help me?" I asked, swallowing hard.

"Why wouldn't I help you?"

"Because you've been following me around for years now to kill me. Now, suddenly, you've come to my rescue?"

"Raven, I have never wanted to kill you. I used to want to marry you, yes. I will not deny this. It was very heart-breaking to be promised something, only to have you run away *forever* on the night of what would have been our wedding. I didn't understand why I wasn't good enough for you."

"I told you that I wanted to marry my mate," I insisted.

"Yes, well. I can understand why. You see, I have recently met mine."

"You have?" It was hard to believe that the universe

would have mated Milos to anyone. It seemed cruel—unless his mate was equally as cruel.

"Yes, and there is no love like the love I feel for my mate," Milos replied with a nod.

"I'm confused. If you have a mate, then why did you crash my wedding?" I asked.

"I didn't realize that was what we were doing. That was all Iris's idea. She was rather obsessed with you. She wanted to be you, all because she knew that I had once loved you." He shrugged. "I'm glad she's gone now. That bitch was crazy."

As he began to cut the ropes off my hands, I asked, "If you have a mate, then why are you even here? How do you know where I am?"

"The only reason I've followed you around at all over the past six months is because I wanted to warn you about Queen Lydia. I knew that she was gearing up to do something crazy." His black eyes met mine. "She's planning to kill you once she gets back to the barn, you know."

"She is? How do you know that?"

"I heard her talking to Gene. He's her boyfriend," he explained. "He lives back in Wolflandia. They were talking on the phone. And she told him that she planned to weaken you enough, to the point where you won't heal. Then, she planned to cut the baby out of you before murdering you."

He finished cutting my hands free and then began to work on my feet.

"I would have gotten to you sooner, but she's been near the barn most of this time. She finally just left."

"Do you know where the Darken pack is?" I asked.

"They're in a hole not far away from here. Once we've finished here, I will go turn off the sensors she's using in the trap so they can escape, too."

As he freed my feet, I asked, "Why are you being so nice to me?"

"Because I no longer want you in the way I once did," he replied. "And what I did you was pretty horrible. But mostly, I just wanted a kiss from you to ignite the Triangle. I wanted to become more powerful. Now that I've had a taste for power, I no longer care for it as much as I once did," he informed me.

"Wow." I was shocked to hear him say those words. "I feel like my... Kane... I think he craves it more than once did."

"Kane isn't a good guy, Raven. He never has been, and he never will be. Your mother was extremely opposed to you marrying him during the Ancient times, and she wasn't wrong about that. You'd be better off getting away from him, even though I know that won't be easy, all things considered." He pointed his chin at my pregnant stomach.

"Yeah."

"You have to end this war. Everyone is waiting for you to end it," Milos went on.

"How? I don't really know what I'm supposed to do to end it," I admitted. I'd given it so much thought, especially since I had been locked up in this barn, alone with nothing but my thoughts, and I just couldn't seem to figure it out.

"Well, the rest of the paranormal world believes that

the werewolves are the ones who started this," Milos explained.

"Because, technically, they did." And by 'they', I meant him.

He let out a little chuckle. "I suppose we did. So, anyway, all you need to do is get yourself on TV and announce that the war is over, that freedom rings—whatever you want to say. Just let the rest of the paranormal world know that you, the Queen of the wolves, is calling it quits on this war. Your husband should probably be there, too."

"Okay," I agreed with a nod. I would be sure to include Kane in that, right before I most likely kicked him to the curb.

I wasn't sure how the whole curb kicking thing was going to work when our souls were permanently bound together, but I was about to find out.

At that moment, I spotted her out of the corner of my eye: just a flash of light hair.

"Milos, watch out," I said.

He whirled around and pulled the gun out of his pocket so fast it wasn't even funny.

Before he even allowed Queen Lydia to say a word, he fired the gun.

I watched as my mother fell, lifelessly, to the ground.

CHAPTER 24

*K*nowing that Queen Lydia was truly dead, once and for all, was a huge relief.

As I followed Milos to the hole where she had been keeping my mates, I hoped that nothing had happened to any of them.

As we approached the hole, I glanced inside.

I breathed a sigh of relief to find that all three of them were down there, fully alive.

"Raven? You're okay. Thank god you're okay," Aiden called up to me.

"I'm okay. Queen Lydia is dead. Milos killed her when he rescued me from the barn that she has been keeping me in," I told them.

"Here, Raven, have a sandwich." Milos handed me a sandwich wrapped in foil, along with a bottle of water. Even though I normally would have worried that he was trying to poison me or something, he had proved today that he was on my side.

I was willing to let him stay alive when he had proven

himself to be the good guy. Besides, I wasn't sure how much he had even done to try to hurt me in the past. One thing was for sure, though.

The past was the past; I was so ready to focus on the future.

As I opened the foil and then took a bite of the peanut butter and jelly sandwich, I thought about what needed to be done next.

Step #1: Rescue my mates from the hole.

Step #2: End the war.

"Milos is going to turn off the sensors that could kill you, and then you guys can climb out of there," I told them.

"I even have some rope to help lift you," Milos offered as he pressed what looked like a remote control. "Sensors are off."

Tossing the long rope into the hole, Colton grabbed it first. Milos helped lift him out of the hole. Next, Aiden climbed out and then, Rhys.

"Why are you being so cool with us?" Colton asked him.

"I've just had a change of heart." Milos shrugged. "I met my mate. I fell in love. I'm a different person now."

"I kind of like this version of you," Rhys said with a shrug.

"We all do," I agreed.

Who would have thought that, in the end, Milos Santorini would be the one to save our lives?

CHAPTER 25

My mates all transitioned to their werewolf forms as we headed back to the castle. I had never really realized how beautiful each of them looked in their wolf form. It was the little things in life, the things that you appreciated after a near death experience.

Once we made it back to the castle, they all turned back to their human forms. I had a hard time not jumping all of their bones; to say that they looked completely gorgeous naked would have been an understatement.

"You guys, I need your help. How can I arrange to have a speech I want to give aired on television?" I asked.

"Easy. I can get ahold of Luke and have it arranged," Aiden explained. "What are you planning on doing?"

"Ending the war. It was actually Milos's suggestion." I smiled, surprised that I would ever be giving him credit for something.

"When do you want to do this?" Aiden asked.

"In about an hour?" I asked.

"Alright. I'll go charge up my phone and make a call."

"Thank you." I paused for a moment. "Do you think we can arrange for there to be an audience, too?"

"Yeah, I think we can figure that out." He stood there for a moment, his honey brown eyes on mine. "I'm sorry, by the way. I'm sorry that I ever got upset with you before we went hunting."

"Don't apologize," I informed him. "You have every right to feel the way you do about me choosing Aiden. You should know that it's a decision I regret."

I decided not to tell him what I had planned next. I knew it would be better for everyone to all just watch it all unfold.

* * *

ONCE WE WERE inside the castle, I headed straight for the King's Quarters.

The door was unlocked, so I opened it. I found Kane sitting in front of the TV.

"What are you doing?" I asked him.

He turned to me, a look of confusion in his green eyes. "Where have you been for the past few days?"

"Well, since you asked, I was actually kidnapped."

"Kidnapped?" His eyes widened. "By *who*?"

"Queen Lydia."

He shot me a funny look. "She died hundreds of years ago."

"Actually, she didn't. She's been in hiding all of these years," I explained. "She's dead now. Fortunately, I was able to escape from her—no thanks to you."

"Raven, I'm sorry. I had no idea you were kidnapped," he said quietly.

"Where did you think I went?" I asked him.

"Honestly? I thought you were upset about our fight and ran away because of it," he explained.

I suppressed an eye roll. "Well, I didn't. It hurts to know that you didn't even bother to look for me."

"I'm really sorry, Raven." Even though he said the words, the truth was that he didn't really even *look* sorry; it was as if he just knew that he was supposed to apologize, but his voice completely lacked emotion.

"I need you to do something for me," I told him.

"Sure, what is it?" Kane asked.

"I need you to get dressed and then meet me in about an hour. I want you to meet me on the platform where our crowns are. I want to sit on them. Do you think you can do that?" I asked him.

"Sure, but why?"

"I want to feel the power of sitting upon our thrones. I want to know how it feels."

His eyes slid over to meet mine as a smile crept onto his face.

"That's my girl." He leaned in and kissed me on the lips.

I kissed him back, knowing that it was all just an act on my part at this point.

"Oh, one other thing. Wear your crown for me, too, okay?" I asked him.

"Of course, my Queen."

* * *

I HEADED to my room and got ready. To say that I was nervous would have been an understatement.

I knew that I couldn't tell Kane what I was about to do, because I was certain that he would fight me over it. He wouldn't want to end this war—even if I begged him to.

But I also knew that no one would take it seriously unless we were *both* there to address the entire paranormal world. That was the downside of the patriarchal paranormal society we lived in. A Queen's address alone just wouldn't be enough.

Well, I had a plan.

I just hoped that it would work.

CHAPTER 26

J got to our thrones before Kane did. That gave me just the right amount of time to do what needed to be done for this to work out.

"Silenti audioso for Kane's ears only upon his arrival," I whispered, hoping that it would work. If Kane wasn't able to hear my address, then there was nothing he would be able to do to stop it in the moment. And that was all I needed: to end the war with him by my side... *without him knowing what was going on.*

This plan seemed too good to be true. I was afraid that it wouldn't work.

Glancing out in the crowd, I noticed that there was a fairly large audience already sitting there, waiting to see what my address would be.

It hadn't taken much time for Aiden to round up an audience for me.

I hadn't really cared about there being an audience, but that was how it had all played out in Gloria's vision. I wanted to keep it as accurate to her vision as possible.

The other Darken all approached the platform where I was already sitting upon my throne, wearing my crown.

"I want the cameraman to go under an invisibility spell," I told them. "Do you think we can arrange that?"

"An invisibility spell? Why?" Colton asked with raised eyebrows.

"Because Kane has no idea what I'm about to do. I've already done a spell so he won't hear anything when he arrives, but I just realized that he'll see the cameraman, too—unless we make him invisible."

"Kane is going to flip out when he realizes you've gone to so many extremes just to hide from him that you're ending the war," Aiden said. "Are you sure you want to go through with this?"

"Yes," I replied with a nod. I had never been more certain about anything before in my life.

"Okay. The camera guy is here now," Colton said, pointing his chin at a guy who was walking in our direction. "I'll go tell him why we need him to become invisible."

"Thanks, Colton."

As Colton and Rhys both headed in the camera guy's direction, Aiden glanced over at me. "You're a beautiful Queen. Have I told you that?"

"Thanks," I replied with a smile.

At that moment, I felt a cramp in my stomach. It passed just as quickly as I'd felt it come on.

"I mean it, Raven. You're beautiful *and* powerful." His honey brown eyes met mine. "I'm so proud of everything you've accomplished so far. And I'm so proud of you for coming up with this scheme to end the war without Kane knowing. It's the right thing to do."

"Let's just hope it works," I replied quietly. Even though I knew that I was doing everything I possibly could to make this happen, there was this doubt in the back of my mind that told me that something wasn't going to go according to plan.

I chalked it up to nerves. I was about to trick my husband—my King—into doing something I knew he wouldn't want to do. Anyone in my situation would have been nervous and maybe a little bit paranoid.

At that moment, I spotted Kane walking over to us.

Glancing over at Colton and Rhys, who were standing center of the stage, I breathed a huge sigh of relief. The camera guy was no longer invisible, so I knew that they had already placed him under an invisibility spell.

I remembered that in Gloria's vision, I had begun my address before Kane walked onto the stage. So, that was exactly what I was going to do.

"Ready, set, record," I announced to the camera guy.

"Rolling," he called out to me.

I began my speech. "Ladies and gentlemen across all of the paranormal societies, I have an announcement to make to you. King Kane and I have made a decision today, one that affects all of us." I forced a smile for the camera. "It is with great pride that I announce to you that the war has ended. While we mourn the deaths of the ones we have lost, we are relieved that more lives weren't taken from us. I promise you that, during my reign, we will never see a war as ugly as the one we are now free of."

JAYME MORSE & JODY MORSE

At that moment, Kane walked across the stage, wearing his crown atop his head.

As he sat down on his throne next to me, he looked completely confused. I hadn't warned him that there would be an audience.

But he also didn't look like he was confused in a bad way, either. I was pretty sure that he was happy to find that there were so many people there, watching him sit on his throne and wear his crown.

"Going forward, we will see some changes happening." I darted my eyes over at Kane to see if he could hear what I was saying, but he was looking in the other direction— completely oblivious that I had spoken. I beamed, relieved that my spell had worked. "First of all, I ask that all battles going on right now stop immediately. Please cease fire." I paused. "Once there have been no more battles, I want us to resume life as usual. Workplaces will reopen, and schools will resume, including Werewolf Academy and Lupin Academy," I announced.

People cheered from the audience.

I noticed Kane wave at the crowd. I tried hard not to chuckle at the fact that he thought they were cheering at us sitting upon our thrones.

I felt something again then: pain radiating through me. Something wasn't right.

"I will have more updates to come. That is all for now. Thank you for listening to this address." Then, without saying another word, I rose from the throne and hurried off the platform.

Glancing over my shoulder, I was surprised to find that Kane was actually following after me. I would have expected him to continue to drink up all of the attention he was getting.

As I reached the door that led into the rest of the castle, I found myself hunching over in pain in the hallway.

"Raven, is everything alright?" Kane asked from behind me.

I felt the waves rippling through my core. They started out lightly before intensifying; they were extremely close together—only seconds apart.

I knew that they were contractions.

I glanced down at my stomach, realizing how much more pregnant I looked than I had just days ago. Somehow, this baby had managed to thrive, even while we were being starved by the Queen.

A contraction hit me then; it was strong and painful enough to make me yelp.

"Raven?" Kane whispered.

Glancing over at him, I said, "The baby's coming."

"Uh," Kane said, his eyes wide. "It's coming *now*?"

"Yes," I hissed at him through another contraction.

I felt water trickling down my legs.

"Your water just broke," he commented. "There should be enough time for us to get you to… to Gloria."

"I don't think there's enough time." My face twisted with the pain that shot through me. "I don't know what to do. I need help," I groaned out through gritted teeth.

"You think I have any idea what to do?" Kane asked, an angered expression on his face.

I couldn't believe he was fighting with me right now.

I shouldn't have been so surprised.

But this wasn't about him and how much of a jerk he was being. I needed to figure out how to get this baby out of me without us both dying.

Could a werewolf even die during labor? If the baby could have killed me while it was inside of me, I was pretty sure that it could have killed me while it was trying to make its way out of me—but I wasn't sure.

I started walking down the hallway, in the direction of one of the closest bedrooms.

"Where are you going?" Kane questioned my turned back.

"Where do you think, Kane? Queens do not give birth to their babies on the floor."

But it was already too late. My body didn't care that I was a Queen. It had other plans. As I started to push involuntarily, I fell to my knees on the marble tiled floor.

I wasn't sure how much longer I had.

When I caught a glimpse of Kane's face, I couldn't help but notice that he looked a little disgusted. Or maybe he was grossed out about the fact that I was about to give birth to our little Prince or Princess right there in the middle of the hallway. Either way, he turned away from me so he didn't have to watch what would happen next.

At that moment, I felt a pair of strong arms lifting me up.

As I glanced up into his dark blue eyes, I said, "Rhys. I need you."

I didn't speak the rest of my thoughts out loud: *"I need you, because I don't want to give birth with Kane."*

I didn't want him there.

I wanted my other mates, too. Every single one of them.

"I know, baby. That's why I'm here," Rhys said as he carried me into the bedroom and laid me down on the bed.

"Have you ever delivered a baby before?" I managed to grunt out.

"Yes, I have. I used to be a doctor, about twenty years ago."

I felt a huge sense of relief, knowing I was in good hands.

My other mates came into the room then.

Colton grabbed my left hand, as Aiden moved around to the other side of me and grabbed my right hand.

"I need you to push for me, Raven," Rhys told me.

And so, I did.

I screamed out in pain the entire time.

"We've almost got him."

Him. Queen Lydia had been right.

"One more big push," Rhys instructed.

I pushed with everything I had.

A moment later, I heard the baby crying and then watched as Rhys took him away to clean him off.

I laid back on the bed, completely exhausted.

"Uh, Raven," Rhys said as he handed me the baby. "I really don't think this is Kane's baby."

"What do you mean?" I let out a little laugh.

But then I stared down into the baby's face, and I realized exactly what he meant.

The baby's black hair and striking bright blue eyes instantly told me right away that this baby wasn't Kane's.

He was Theo's.

I hadn't only been pregnant for six months; I had been pregnant nearly an entire year.

And suddenly, everything began to make sense. The baby hadn't been mad at me that night it had tried to kill me. I was pretty sure that this baby had somehow known that Kane was Theo's enemy and that he was bad for me—bad *for us.*

And when I had seen Theo in the garden that night, the reason the baby had been so excited inside my stomach was because he had known that it was his father. I wasn't sure how he knew, but he had known. I supposed that it was probably because he was a direct Descendant from two Ancients; having such a powerful bloodline, his magical abilities may have even been stronger than my own.

I wished, more than anything, that I could tell Theo.

Even more than that, I wished that I could tell the other Darken that Theo was still alive, but I had sworn myself to secrecy.

"Raven, are you okay?" Colton asked me, his gray eyes meeting mine with a sense of worry.

I glanced up at him. "I couldn't be happier."

"Why hasn't Kane come in to see the baby yet?" Rhys questioned. "He doesn't even know it's not his yet."

"I think he got squeamish." I shrugged. "I really don't want him to come in to see him, if we're being honest. I'd rather not deal with him right now. I just want to be surrounded by the ones I really love." I glanced around at my mates with a smile.

"So, uh, what are you naming him?" Aiden asked me.

I considered it for a moment. "I like Austin."

"Hi, Prince Austin." Aiden reached out and grabbed his little baby hand.

I smiled.

Everything in this world was right.

Theo's words echoed through my mind then. *"This is all going to make sense one day."*

CHAPTER 27

I must have fallen asleep at some point. When I woke up, I noticed that there was a crib alongside me. The Darken must have left Austin there before leaving the room.

"Knock, knock," Maddie called out. I glanced over at the doorway to find her and Vince standing there.

"Congratulations, honey," Vince said as they entered the room. "We heard the news—and the really good news."

I knew what he meant: that the baby wasn't Kane's.

I was pretty sure that we *all* thought that was good news.

"Thank you. Do you want to hold him?" I asked, climbing out of bed and scooping Austin up.

I might have only been imagining it, but I could have sworn that he had already grown a few pounds since I had given birth a few hours ago. I knew that werewolf babies grew really quickly—much quicker than human babies did, but I hadn't been expecting that.

"Of course we do," Maddie said with a smile as I placed her into his arms. "Hi, Austin. I'm your Aunt Maddie."

"And I'm your Uncle Vince," he cooed.

"We saw your address on TV," Maddie said, glancing over me then as she cradled Austin in her arms. "I can't believe Kane let you end the war."

"Actually, he doesn't know I did," I admitted. "I tricked him."

"How did you manage to pull *that* off?" Vince asked with wide eyes.

"Oh, you know. Just a little magic." I paused for a moment and then told them, "So much has happened this week, you guys. I was kidnapped—"

"By who?" Maddie's eyes widened.

"Queen Lydia—my biological mother," I explained.

"I thought she was dead!" Vince said.

"She was supposed to be." I paused for a moment. "She is now. You won't believe who killed her when he helped rescue me."

"Who?" Maddie's eyes widened.

"Milos. We're, like, *friends* now."

"What? You and Milos Santorini are friends?" Vince just stared back at me like I was an alien. "Who are you and what have you done with Raven?"

I laughed. "As it turns out, a lot of things we thought he did, Queen Lydia was behind. For example, she's the one who shot Theo during our first year at Werewolf Academy."

"Wow. So, you and Milos are just... cool now? Or do you still want to get your revenge eventually?"

"He was the villain," Vince reminded me.

"He met his mate. It seems like he really changed him —even *with* the Triangle ignited. I don't know. He seems okay. Who knows what the future will bring? But I honestly don't think he's going to be a problem for me anymore. He saved my life. The Queen was planning to kill me... after stealing Austin."

"Wow. What a wicked bitch," Vince commented.

That was one way to put it.

"We'll forever be grateful for him for saving your life. I have to send him a fruit basket," Maddie said.

"You think a fruit basket is equal to our Raven's life?" Vince asked her.

"Obviously not, but we should do something nice for him for saving her," Maddie explained.

I laughed. "So, uh, there's something else I need to tell you guys."

"What is it?" Vince glanced over at me. I was pretty sure that he was almost afraid of what I was about to say next, considering I had just told them Milos was my friend.

I swallowed hard. "She's not the only one who's still alive, either. If I tell you guys this, can you promise to keep it a secret from my mates?"

"When do we *ever* spill the beans?" Vince asked.

"Seriously. We're, like, official secret keepers," Maddie added.

I smiled. "Sorry. It's just that I promised not to tell the rest of the Darken. He didn't want them to know."

"Who's 'he'?" Maddie asked.

"Theo."

Her jaw dropped, and Vince gasped.

"He's alive?" Vince asked.

"Yeah. I saw him in the garden," I replied with a nod. "He faked his own death. He even went to the extent of using magic to make our mate bond to make it believable to me."

"But why would he do that?" Maddie asked.

"I don't know yet. He wouldn't tell me the reason. He told me that it will all make sense eventually and that he'll come back to me. And well, now that he has a child, I hope he'll come back sooner rather than later." I paused for a moment and then told them, "I know this is going to sound crazy, but the baby was excited to see him before he was even born. I could just *feel* it. And he hated Kane. Gloria thought Austin was trying to kill me, but I'm pretty sure he was actually trying to kill Kane."

"Well, this kid is an incredible judge of character then," Vince said as held Austin. "Yes, you are. We all hate Kane. You're now an honorary member of the She-Man-Kane-Haters-Club."

I snorted.

"So, now that the war is over, I guess we'll be leaving soon," Maddie said, glancing over at me. "It's safe for us to go back to Wolflandia again."

"We'll be going back to Werewolf Academy now that you've reopened it."

I nodded. "That's why I reopened it. It's time for students to go back and continue their education."

"What about you?" Vince asked.

"Well, I guess I have to focus on being a Queen… and a mom." I shrugged.

I wasn't going to lie; it made me a little sad that my

friends would be leaving, but I knew it wasn't forever. I was sure that they would visit me when they could, and I would make the trip to Wolflandia. We still had the house near the school that we could stay at whenever we wanted.

Besides, I had my mates here, too.

All of my mates... *even Kane, unfortunately.*

CHAPTER 28

*W*hen I settled back into the Queen's Quarters with Prince Austin, we fell into a routine. Werewolf babies, even from the day they were born, were far more hyper and energetic than human babies. To say that he had been keeping me busier than I even expected would have been an understatement.

Every time I looked at him, all I could see was Theo. To be honest, it gave me hope—hope that Theo would return sooner, rather than later.

I couldn't wait for my mate to meet his son.

In the meantime, all three of my original mates took turns babysitting Austin for me when I needed some free time. Each of them spent a lot of time bonding with Austin.

I knew that they saw what I did when they looked at Austin: Theo.

It made it all the more difficult not to tell them that he was alive, that he would be back again someday.

* * *

I WAS SLEEPING one night when I heard the sound of footsteps.

When I woke up, I saw Kane hovering over the baby's crib with a dagger in his hand.

A sterling silver dagger.

I was on my feet and in his face quicker than you could count to one.

"What the fuck do you think you're doing?" I growled at him.

He grabbed me by the throat and pinned me down onto my bed. "I heard this baby wasn't mine. I had to see for myself. As it turns out, everyone was right. Not only is this creature not mine, it's my enemy's." His eyes flashed with anger. "I can't be letting my wife have a baby that belongs to my enemy, now, can I? I can't have my enemy's son become the next King of the werewolves. I'll have none of this."

"Let go of me," I gasped out, finding it difficult to breathe.

I struggled against him, but he was stronger than me.

Why had I thought I could attack one of the Triangle? Of course he was stronger than me.

Finally, he let go of my throat. "I was going to kill your baby, but I think it might be easier for me to just kill *both* of you at this point. I know you tricked me into ending the war. That was incredibly fucked up."

"What's incredibly fucked up is the fact that you wanted to marry me just to become King," I replied, trembling beneath him. I wasn't sure what he was planning to do, but I was a little too nervous to find out.

His green eyes stared into mine menacingly. "If I get rid of both of you, I will be the only ruler of the werewolf race, and I will call *all* of the shots." It seemed like he was thinking out loud to himself. "Yeah, I think that's what I'll do."

As he raised the dagger into the air, I saw a movement from behind him.

It took me a moment to realize that someone else was in here with us.

I watched as he tiptoed across the room, sneaking up on Kane. That was when I saw his wave of black hair, and his blue eyes locked on mine from feet away.

It was Theo.

Theo had returned.

So many emotions washed over me: relief, excitement, confusion, but most of all... fear. Fear that he was about to get caught up in something bad.

When I glanced back over at Kane, I saw that he still had the dagger raised in the air. It looked like he was about to drive it into my heart.

I crawled backwards, further away from him on the bed, knowing that the dagger would end my life; I knew that it was made from sterling silver, just like a bullet.

Just as I had put some distance between us, I heard the sound of the gun being fired.

Kane slumped over onto the foot of the bed.

Theo scooped the dagger up. I breathed a slight sigh of relief.

I knew that a silver bullet wasn't enough to kill Kane—especially coming from Theo.

Since he was a part of the Triangle, it was up to *me* to kill him.

I had to use magic.

The elements were what killed the Triangle, I remembered.

I thought for a moment before envisioning that Kane would get hit by lightning. A moment later, a lightning bolt touched down inside the room, shooting straight through him.

I heard the sound of his body being zapped with an electrical surge.

That was when I heard him stop breathing, and I felt it.

Our mate bond was severed. I could tell that something had happened, but the strange part was that it didn't hurt the way my mate bond being cut with Theo had hurt. I didn't even feel sad; it just felt a little weird.

"He's dead," I whispered as I moved to stand next to Theo. "Thank you for saving me."

"Don't thank me," Theo said, shaking his head. "I would be lost without you, Raven."

"How did you even get here?" His timing had been impeccable.

"I heard your thoughts, Raven. I guess you took the locket off."

I reached for my neck and realized that it was gone. One of my mates must have taken it off of me when I had given birth and put it somewhere for safekeeping. I hadn't even noticed it until right now.

"I know that Austin's my son," Theo went on. "I just knew I couldn't stay away from you any longer. I had to come see you and meet him."

"Are you back for good?" I asked him.

"Yes. I promise I'll never leave you again." He wrapped his arms around me and then brought his mouth down on mine.

Once we broke our kiss, I scooped Austin up from his crib and handed him to Theo.

"Hi, Austin." Theo was beaming. I had never seen him so happy in his life. "I'm your daddy."

Austin cooed and smiled; I had yet to see him look so happy before, either. I hated to think of what could have happened just moments before, if Theo hadn't arrived just in the nick of time.

I tried to push the thought to the back of my mind. It was over now. Kane was gone forever.

Now the Darken could go back to normal… or as close to normal as it could ever get, after everything our pack had been through.

"We need to do something about his body." I pointed my chin at Kane's corpse. "I want it out of my bed."

"Let's go bury it," Theo said.

"Okay." I took the baby back from him. "I'm going to go ask Maddie to watch Austin."

I had a feeling this was going to be a really, really long night.

* * *

Fifteen minutes later, we had a hole dug out. As it turned out, werewolves were really fast grave diggers. Who knew?

Once it was dug, Theo tossed Kane's body into a hole in the ground and we began to pile dirt on top of it.

"I'm so relieved to close this chapter of my life—the one with *him* in it." I gave Kane's face one final glance before covering it with dirt.

"Me, too. Knowing that you were with him every day... Well, it scared the shit out of me." His blue eyes met mine. "Kane is the reason I faked my own death, Raven."

"Why? I don't understand."

"Gloria showed me a vision, too." His eyes met mine. "I saw this very moment, in fact."

"You saw that you would sneak into the Queen's Quarters to stop him from killing me?" I asked.

"No. I saw the two of us burying his body," he explained. "She told me that I needed to fake my own death, but here's the thing. She told me that I had to do it with the help of Headmaster Crane. He helped me devise a plan to kill Kane. There's something you don't know about Headmaster Crane."

"What?" I asked with raised eyebrows.

"He's Kane's father," Theo explained. "And no one—I mean, *no one*—in this world hated Kane as much as Headmaster Crane did."

"Why would he hate his own son?" I asked him.

"Kane killed his mother, leaving Headmaster Crane heartbroken for years." He paused for a moment. "Don't get me wrong. I don't like Headmaster Crane himself. But he's gone now."

"Gone?"

"Dead. He died of a broken heart when his mate died the other day. His mate was Lydia," Theo informed me.

"You knew she was alive?" I asked with raised eyebrows.

"Not until after he died. I went through his wallet, and I saw her pictures."

"Wow. Wait. Werewolves can die of a broken heart when their mate dies?" I questioned.

"Yeah," Theo nodded.

"Why didn't I die from a broken heart when I thought I lost you?" That had been the worst pain I had ever experienced in my life.

"Well, I think part of it was because you had your other mates to lean on. You had four other mates that took up a part of your heart."

"True."

"I also think that fate knew we would be together again one day." His blue eyes met mine.

I smiled up at him. "I just wish that we didn't have so much time apart."

"Me, too." He swallowed hard. "Gloria also saw the alternative. She saw what would have happened if I didn't fake my own death. If I faked my death, then I would be able to come back and we would bury Kane one day. But if I didn't fake my own death... Well, that vision she showed me just about killed me."

"What was it?" I asked him.

"Gloria showed me my own funeral. She showed me you crying at it. The reason I died was because Kane killed me in order to become King."

"So, basically, even *if* you stuck around, Kane was going to end up being King at some point, anyway. The only difference was that you wouldn't have been alive to find out about it if you had stuck around."

"Yup." He nodded.

"You did the right thing, Theo. I'm not mad at you for faking your own death. At all. I wish I had been able to know, but maybe it was better that I was in the dark about it. I don't know." I sighed. "All I know is that I'm so glad you're back for good."

"Me, too, baby." His eyes met mine and then he kissed me again.

"I want you," I whispered when we broke the kiss.

"I want you, too." He paused. "Why don't you go meet me in the Queen's Quarters? I'll be up there in a second."

"Okay," I agreed with a nod.

As I headed towards the castle, my heart pounded with every step.

I had craved him with every ounce of my being for so long now. I was finally about to have him—every part of him—again, and that was overwhelming.

CHAPTER 29

When I opened the door to the Queen's Quarters, I was shocked to find that Theo was already inside waiting for me.

"How did you even beat me here?" I asked him.

His bright blue eyes locked on mine. "Easy. I move fast when I want something badly enough."

As I glanced around the room, I realized that he hadn't just beat me here; he had somehow managed to light candles throughout the room and scatter rose petals everywhere. I wasn't sure where he had even gotten them, but my guess was that he must have picked them from the garden.

"Raven, you have no idea how much I've missed you. I haven't just missed you. I've completely craved you. Ever since that night in the garden when our mate bond was reignited, I've wanted nothing more than to see you again. And touch you." He reached out and touched my cheek gently. "And kiss you."

His lips came crashing down on mine. His mouth felt

fiery hot against my own. He kissed me hungrily, in a way that he had never kissed me before.

Pulling my dress off over my head, he broke our kiss and stared me up and down. His eyes drifted over my body, lingering on the lacy black panties and matching bra I was wearing.

I couldn't control myself any longer, I reached for his belt and undid it.

As his pants dropped to the floor, I pulled his shirt off over his head.

He unhooked my bra, tossing it to the floor and then lifted me into his arms. With one swift motion, he tossed me onto the bed.

I had never seen him want me so badly. The desire was obvious in his eyes and in his movements.

Climbing onto the bed, he kissed me again and then began to plant a trail of kisses down my neck. He dragged his lips downwards, stopping to suck each nipple gently, eliciting soft moans from me.

"God damn, I want you so bad, baby. It's been too long," he murmured as he continued to kiss his way down my stomach.

Parting my thighs, he pulled my panties down over my knees and tossing them to the floor, leaving me completely exposed to him.

His sparkling blue eyes met mine.

"Tell me what you want, Raven," he said as he rested his hand on my upper thigh.

"I want you," I whispered.

"What do you want me to do to you?"

"I want you to touch me," I managed to whisper, my

craving for him taking over.

His hand moved upwards, his fingers grazing ever so lightly over my slit.

A shiver crept its way down my spine at his touch.

"More?" he asked.

I nodded.

He touched me then, pushing two fingers inside of me.

My whole body shook at his touch. He had never shown this side of himself to me before, but whatever it was… my body was reacting well to it. I had never been wetter in my life.

"Tell me what you really want. Raven." His blue eyes were on mine again, daring me to tell him what I wanted.

"I want you to lick me."

His eyes locked on mine. "Where?"

"My pussy." I swallowed hard and then whispered, "Please."

Dipping his head, he licked me… just once.

My thighs began to shake.

Grabbing his hair, I pulled his head into me.

His tongue swirled its way around my pussy, and then he began to flick his tongue against my clit.

A moan escaped my mouth. I couldn't take it much longer. I could already feel it building up. Gripping his head, I felt my legs beginning to quiver and my breathing growing ragged.

As his mouth clamped down on my clit, sucking it hard, I felt myself come completely undone. A loud moan shuddered from my mouth.

As my breathing returned to normal, he shifted

himself so that he was hovering above me. He began to kiss my neck again.

"Now, tell me what you want," I said, making eye contact with him.

"To be inside of you," Theo whispered, staring out at me from behind his fiery, blue-eyed gaze.

"Fuck me," I whispered.

His lips came crashing down hard on mine then as I spread my legs for him, wrapping them around his waist.

He gently pushed his tip against my entrance, teasing me. Then, with one slow movement, he pushed himself inside of me.

I gasped as he entered me.

He began to move in me slowly at first—too slowly.

Wrapping my legs around his waist, I pulled him deeper into me.

As he began to move faster and harder, building up to a steady rhythm, I found myself moaning and whimpering against his mouth.

My body began to tremble as he whispered, "Come with me."

I felt myself constricting around him as his breathing became heavy. I moaned out his name as I came completely undone. Seconds later, I felt his warm release.

As Theo slumped on top of me, he whispered, "I love you, Raven Gallagher."

"I love you, too, Theo Rossi," I whispered back.

* * *

THEO and I laid in silence in each other's embrace for the longest time. With moonlight streaming in through the open window and the lit candles that he had placed throughout the room, everything about this night felt perfect.

It was more than just perfect.

For the first time in a long time, I felt complete.

It felt like Theo was the missing piece of the puzzle that I had been trying to put together for such a long time now. Now that he had returned, everything felt right again—the way it should have been all along.

"Do you hear that?" Theo asked me.

I realized that it had started to rain then. I took in the soft pitter patter of the raindrops on the stone castle. I had always loved the sound of rain; I loved it even more in this moment.

"It's raining," I murmured.

He shook his head. "No, that's not what I meant. Listen closer."

I listened for a moment, and that was when I heard it.

His heart was beating, completely in sync with mine.

But the thing was, it wasn't only his heartbeat that I could hear.

I could hear all four of my mates' heartbeats, loud and clear. They were all beating in sync with mine. But the thing was, I couldn't pick out their heart beats individually; it was just that instinctively I knew that I could hear all of their heartbeats.

"All *five* of our hearts are beating together in harmony." I glanced down at my wrist, noticing that my Darken pack tattoo had returned to normal. "And my tattoo went back to how it used to be. After I married Kane, it looked shattered, but now it looks the same way it did before." My eyes darted over to meet Theo's. "What could that even mean?"

"I'm not sure. All I know is that it must mean *something.*"

Deep down, I had a suspicion of my own. I wondered if the reason I had never heard the Darken members' hearts beating continuously since I had become mated to all of them had something to do with Kane. Maybe it had never been destiny for him to be my mate, or for him to be a part of our pack, in general. Maybe him being alive had somehow prevented me from having the full mate bond with the rest of the Darken, and now that he was gone, our mate connections had strengthened.

A part of me wanted to tell Theo about my theory, but I decided to keep it to myself. I knew that moving onto the next chapter of our lives—the chapter *without* Kane— was to bury the memories of him. And the first step to doing that was to stop talking about him.

We needed to all forget that he had ever existed. I knew that wouldn't happen overnight or even in the near future, but in five or ten years from now, I didn't want to have to be reminded of him again.

Mostly, what I wanted was to go back to my old life. The life that I had lived—and loved—before I had ever even known that Kane existed. The life I had lived before this war had ever begun.

I turned to Theo then. "Now that the war is over and all of my enemies are gone, there's something I want more than *anything.*"

"What is it?" His striking blue eyes sparkled under the dim lighting as they pierced straight through mine.

"Well, actually, there are two things. The first," I said, staring up into his face, "is to marry you."

"Did you just propose to me?" Theo asked, his eyebrows lifting questioningly as a smile crept onto his lips.

"Sort of," I replied.

"Well, I guess I did sort of propose to you on Christmas a year ago," he reminded me.

I laughed, smiling at the memory.

"Why this sudden decision to marry me now?" Theo asked.

"Well, I would have married you a while ago now that you're alive."

"Instead, you married Kane." There was a slightly bitter edge to his tone. I knew then that forgetting about Kane was going to be even harder for all of us than I had originally realized.

"I married Kane because I had to. I know you've missed so much while you were gone. But here's the thing. Paranormal law said that I couldn't become Queen unless I took a husband. That was the reason I married Kane. I'm not saying that I didn't love Kane at one point, but I got married to him because I had to. I viewed it as a contract." I paused for a moment. "There's another part of the law, though—one that's affecting me now. Paranormal law says that there has to be a King at *all* times, or I must step down from the throne."

"That's a completely barbaric law," Theo said, shaking

his head. "You are more than capable to be Queen, with or without a King."

"I know," I replied.

"You should try to use your Queenly powers to change the law," he suggested.

"Maybe I will… someday. Things eventually need to change. But right now, I am accepting that this is a patriarchal realm that we live in, and some things just won't change overnight. The last thing I want is for the crown to fall into the wrong hands. We were already way too close to that happening. I can't let anyone stand in the way. I vowed to protect the werewolf race, and that's exactly what I will do. But in order to do that, I have no choice but to get married again."

"So, what you're saying is that you're only proposing to me because you *have* to get married—not because you *want* to get married."

"I do have to get married, yes. But even *if* it wasn't the law, I still want you to be my King."

"Why me?"

"Because I love you," I told him.

"I love you, too. But this is about more than just love. Why do you want me to be your King?" Theo pressed.

"Because together, we just work." I tried to put it into words. "There's just something about you and me that makes sense. I have to choose someone to rule alongside me for the rest of my life, and I want it to be you. I believe it was always meant to be you." I met his eyes. "The day you faked your own death, I planned to choose you, Theo. I was about to tell you that I chose you and then I heard the gunshot and felt our mate bond being broken."

Pausing for a moment, I quietly added, "It just about killed me."

He studied my face for a long moment.

"What about the others?" he finally asked.

"I don't know. I still love them and care about them deeply, but it's you who I want to be at my side while I reign." I paused for a moment before adding, "And you made it very clear that I couldn't choose all of you years ago, so it's not like there's much to think about here. I had to choose one of you, and I choose you."

I had always known that I would end up here one day, choosing only one of them for good. I hadn't expected it all to happen the way it would, but one thing was for sure.

It had been one hell of a ride.

I had made so many good memories with all of my mates. Even though I could only choose one now that it all came down to it, I wished that I could choose them all.

"Raven, there's something I want to say." Theo's blue eyes locked on mine. "I've done a lot of reflection since the two of us have been apart, and I've given this whole arrangement a lot of thought. And the truth is that if you don't want to make a decision between the four of us... I understand."

"You do?" That was the absolute last thing I had been expecting him to say.

"Yeah, I'm okay with it. I would rather have you and share you with the others than not have you at all."

"Why the change of heart?" I was just so surprised that he had changed his mind about all of this. For so long, he had been so insistent about the fact that I needed to make a decision between the Darken, that I couldn't choose to be with all of them.

"I'm afraid that the pain of losing three mate bonds might be enough to actually kill you," he admitted quietly, stroking my hair. "And even though this arrangement isn't what any of us had planned from the beginning, I think we can make it work. Actually, let me rephrase that. We *will* make it work, if this is what you want."

I thought about it. Ever since the first night I had learned Theo was still alive, I had really thought he was the one who I would end up choosing. I had believed it would be me and him in the end—just the two of us. The idea of not choosing between the four of them hadn't even seemed like an option.

Was it possible for me to be with all four of them?

I could only marry one of them, of course. Paranormal law stated that there could only be one King and one Queen; polyamorous relationships were off-limits when it came to the royal thrones.

But, then again, maybe that was something I could try to change the law about over time, too. After all, it wasn't *my* fault I had ended up with four mates.

"I have to think about it," I admitted quietly. There were so many things to consider. I had to make sure that this was what the others even wanted. For all I knew, they might not have been as okay with it as Theo now seemed to be.

"Okay. Think about it all you need to, my love." Theo kissed my knuckles. "You said there were two things you wanted more than anything. What was the second thing?"

I stared into his eyes. "To go home."

I knew that I didn't even need to explain what I meant by that. Judging from the look in Theo's eyes, he already knew.

The Darken house and Werewolf Academy.

As much as the Darken themselves were home, the truth was that the house we had all once shared and the Academy felt like home, too. Even though I had the castle and Nocturne Island, the truth was that my heart longed for home. I wanted to go back to the way life had been before all of this had happened—before I had lost Theo and the war had begun.

Pulling me in closer to him, Theo kissed me on the forehead. "Then let's go home, baby."

CHAPTER 30

"*R*aven Gallagher," Headmistress Wickburn announced into the loudspeaker.

I climbed the stairs that led to the platform and then walked across the stage. My biggest fear was that I was going to trip and fall in front of *everyone*.

Luckily, I didn't.

Caroline Wickburn beamed at me as I approached the podium she was standing behind. I accepted my high school diploma from her. "Congratulations," she said with a grin.

"Thanks." I smiled back at her.

The truth was that graduating from Werewolf Academy hadn't been the easiest feat. We'd had to hire a full-time nanny to watch Austin while I went back to school and all of my mates went back to teaching again. But, somehow, we had managed to pull it all off.

I could hear the applause from the crowd as I continued my way across the stage. Uncle Ryan whistled from the crowd, and all of my mates cheered for me.

Receiving my high school diploma from Werewolf Academy had been a goal I was never sure I would actually accomplish over the past year. I hadn't even been sure if I would end up making it out of the war alive. I was so relieved to have finally made it here—for *all* of the Darken to have made it here, all in one piece.

Everyone except for Kane, that was. There were times when thinking about him made my heart ache a little. He had taken up a special place in my heart, even if it was only meant to be temporary. I knew that, in the long run, we were all so much better off without him. He may have been my mate and someone who I had once loved, but I could never allow myself to forget that he was also a selfish monster.

I spotted my mates in the crowd then. Theo was holding Austin. Seeing the two of them together made my heart melt.

Actually, seeing all four of my mates with Austin made my heart melt. I had known that each of my mates would make an amazing father, but seeing them with my son proved that to me.

I knew that it was a really ambitious goal and Maddie and Vince both thought I was crazy to even consider it, but I wanted to have a child with each of them one day. I wasn't sure how much more complicated that would make this whole arrangement, but one thing was for sure.

We had an eternity to figure all of that out.

In the meantime, I just wanted to enjoy my time with all of them. After losing Kane, I knew how precious and valuable our time together truly was.

* * *

LATER THAT NIGHT, Theo and I slow danced in the middle of the Werewolf Academy gymnasium where prom was being held.

Werewolf Academy did things a bit backwards compared to the human world. Prom came *after* graduation.

The gym was decorated with an "Under the Stars" theme. But the cool thing here was that the decor wasn't constructed with paper mache or LED lights like typical human high schools. They hadn't come from a home décor store.

The room was decorated with magic.

It looked like an authentic night sky above us, filled with stars and a full moon, which casted its glow on the gymnasium floor.

It was absolutely beautiful.

As the song we had been dancing to came to an end and "Thinking Out Loud" by Ed Sheeran began to play, Theo's bright blue-eyed gaze captured mine.

"The stars, the moon, it all looks stunning," Theo said quietly, repeating the words I had said to him the night of our first date—the night he had taken me to the solarium.

"Just like you," I whispered, giving him the same response that he had given me that night.

He began to spin me in circles then, dipping me low and then kissing me on the lips, right there in the middle of the dance floor—as if we were the only ones in the room.

Butterflies swarmed around inside my stomach just as

much as they had the very first time we kissed beneath the stars.

He's mine. As the thought entered my mind, a giddy feeling rushed through me.

Staring up into his eyes, I noticed how the blue shirt he wore under his tuxedo made his bright blue eyes pop. He had worn it to match the navy-blue prom dress I had picked out for tonight; it was a princess-style dress with a sparkly silver bodice.

As the song came to an end, Rhys approached us. "May I have the honor of this next dance?"

As Theo handed me off to him, he smiled and winked at me.

Turning to face Rhys, I stared up into his smiling face as his arms fell to my waist.

"You look beautiful tonight, Raven," Rhys told me. "Every time I think you can't get any more beautiful, you do."

"Thank you." I wrapped my arms around his neck as we got lost to the beat of "All of You" by John Legend.

Once it came to an end, Rhys headed over to get us some punch at the drinks stand.

Glancing over my shoulder at Aiden and Colton, I knew that both of them were waiting for their turn to slow dance with me. Once they'd had their turn, Theo and I would dance again.

To say that they kept me busy would have been a bit of an understatement. But the thing was, I wouldn't have had it any other way.

Maddie and Vince came over to me then. I glanced over at the drinks station, realizing that both Branden

Mitchell and Julie were filling their cups with punch, too.

"You look so happy tonight," Vince said as they approached me.

"Yeah. I don't think I've ever seen you look this happy in our lives," Maddie added.

"That's because I *am* happy." Everything about me—my mind, body, and soul—felt completely happy and at peace with everything, for once. I was so relieved to know that Austin was safe with the babysitter we had left him with back at the Darken house. There was no more Milos or Kane to worry about. Headmaster Black and Queen Lydia were no longer threats to me.

For the first time since I had learned I was a werewolf, it felt like I had nothing to worry about. It was an incredible feeling.

And it wasn't just that. Being here tonight with all four of my mates... Well, I had never thought we would ever make it here. I thought that Theo, especially, wouldn't make it to my prom. But I had once wondered if any of us would. But now that we were here, everything about my prom night felt *right*.

Even though Headmaster Crane had always made it clear that I wouldn't be able to take even one of the Darken as my prom date since they were my professors, his word clearly no longer held any value now that he was gone. Caroline Wickburn hadn't objected to me taking not just one but *all* of my mates to my prom.

Considering I *was* still the Queen of the wolves, I wasn't sure if she could have told me 'no' even *if* she had wanted to. But she seemed completely understanding of my relationships with my mates.

I knew that there were a lot of werewolves in our kingdom who judged the fact that I had chosen to be with all four of my mates, but honestly?

They could fuck off.

We hadn't chosen this. We had never wished for any of it. It had simply just *happened.* And there had been so many times over the past four years that I had wished I could completely undo it all. I had found myself questioning if it was wrong to love more than one of the Darken at one time. I had questioned if it was ethical or moral. I had even wondered if something was wrong with me for loving more than one guy at once. I had thought that not being with all four of them would make things less complicated, but now I knew that the opposite was actually true. Not being with all four of them would completely complicate everything.

How could I have broken any of their hearts, or my own heart, by choosing only one of them?

I couldn't. It just hadn't felt right. And the truth was, you couldn't just undo what was written in your destiny. You couldn't rewrite what had already been spelled out for you in the stars. At the end of the day, none of this had ever been our choice. So, I hadn't been able to choose between them. I couldn't make a decision when it seemed like fate had wanted me to be with all of them. And the idea of giving up even *one* of them had been enough to crush me.

So, I had done what I wanted to believe anyone in my situation would have done.

I had chosen all of them. And I had brought all *four* of them as my prom dates.

But I knew that this was about way more than just prom. What I had really done was made a commitment to the entire Darken pack.

From here on out, all four of them would be my dates to everything, for the rest of my life.

For the rest of eternity.

* * *

"You know what we have to do, right?" Vince asked.

"Of course," Maddie said with a nod. "It just wouldn't be the same if we didn't."

"It's our tradition," I agreed as we fell into line.

"Our *lifelong* tradition," Maddie added. "We have to keep this tradition going, even when we're no longer Werewolf Academy students."

"So, we have to come to the end of the year festival even when we're no longer students?" Vince shot her a skeptical look.

"Actually, I think that's going to be completely doable. You guys, I have exciting news to share," I told them.

"Ooh, what is it?" Maddie's chocolate brown eyes grew really wide.

"Caroline Wickburn offered me a job. You're looking at the future Advanced Lunar Magic professor," I informed them.

"What? No way. What about Professor Lee?" Vince asked.

"Professor Lee isn't going anywhere. We'll be teaching

different classes. Now that Caroline is Headmistress, she wants to make some changes to the Werewolf Academy's curriculum. Magic is going to be a bigger focus than it once was."

"Congratulations!" Maddie said.

"Yeah, congrats, but I have another question," Vince said. "How are you going to teach? What about being Queen?"

"I'll still be Queen. I'll live on Nocturne Island during the weekends and summer," I explained. "I don't know how long I'll end up teaching here. Will I always be a professor at Werewolf Academy?" I shrugged. "The only thing I do know is that this is where my heart is pulling me right now."

"I'm so excited for you," Maddie said as we climbed onto the Tilt-a-Whirl. Vince and I both climbed onto the ride after her.

"I'm excited for you, too, Professor... Romero?" Vince shot me a wide-eyed glance.

"My request to legally change my name finally kicked in this week, so it's Professor Gallagher... *for now*."

"For now?" Maddie's eyes widened.

"Are you guys ready to be in another royal wedding next month?" I asked. The Paranormal High Court had given me thirty days from the date of my Werewolf Academy graduation to get married again.

I hadn't broken the news to my friends until now because I had been too afraid to jinx it. But now that we were close enough, it seemed safe to share with them.

"Abso-freaking-lutely!" Vince beamed.

"Yes, I'm so excited." Maddie grinned.

"And so excited that it won't be to Kane," Vince added.

"Can I help you with wedding planning again?" Maddie asked.

"Sure, but this time, it's going to be a little bit... different." I paused, unsure of how to break the news. "It took a whole lot of persuasion, but I was able to convince the Paranormal High Court to let me get married to *all* of my mates."

"All *four* of them?" Vince's jaw dropped.

I nodded.

"Honey, that just isn't fair," he complained, rolling his eyes. "Don't get me wrong. I love Julie so much. But what I would give to walk in your shoes for even a day."

"Not me. That seems completely *exhausting*. I can barely keep up with one husband, let alone four," Maddie said with a chuckle. "But if you're marrying all four of them, who gets to be King?"

"Well, this was the part that took the most convincing. All four of them will be King."

Vince's jaw drop. "God. Damn."

As the ride slowly began to spin us into motion, I spotted Theo holding Austin and pointing me out to him.

I smiled and waved.

As the ride began to whip us around faster, I couldn't help but think about how much this ride was like the eternal life that lay before me.

It was about to be filled with inevitable twists and turns, and I couldn't wait to find out what would happen next.

The only thing I *did* know was that it would be with them.

All four of them.
My mates.
The loves of my life.
Until the end of time.

THE END.

TO THE READER

We have had so much fun writing this series. Though this last book was particularly difficult for us to write because we wrote it while we were both sick with COVID and also dealing with our grandfather's death, we hope that you've enjoyed the final chapter. We know we enjoyed writing it. We have fallen in love with every character in this series, and it was difficult to say goodbye to them all. We might have bawled while writing these last few chapters. (Don't tell anyone, though).

Thank you for sticking with Raven during her journey with the Darken pack throughout the series. We hope that you've enjoyed tagging along with her through every twist and turn, every laugh, every heartbreak, every kiss, and everything else she went through.

Thank you all for being so patient in between these releases and for not giving up on the Werewolf Academy series. Thank you all for your reviews and feedback -- we love reading them. And most of all, thanks so much for taking a chance on our series. We appreciate all of you so much more than you know.

Love,

Jayme & Jody

IF YOU ENJOYED WEREWOLF ACADEMY, YOU MIGHT LIKE…

Shifter Academy

Paranormal Academy

Tiger Shifter Academy

Nightshade Vampire Academy

Printed in Great Britain
by Amazon